"That Arena's No Place for You. You'll Get Hurt."

"Oh, now I see. What you mean is the arena's no place for any woman."

"Damn it, I didn't say that," he cried in exasperation.

"No, but you *thought* it. Well, just you listen to me. I'm a grown woman, and you're not my keeper. So just leave me alone!"

"And let you get yourself killed? Nothing doing. What's going on, anyway? How'd you manage to get into the men's roping competition? And why?"

"I can't tell you that."

"You'd better," he threatened. "Because I'm not leaving here till you do."

NORA POWERS

taught English at the college level while working on her Ph.D. A prolific writer, she is the author of some 500 pieces of children's verse, 58 short stories, 9 novels, and various newspaper articles. She has been a published author for the last twenty years and reports, "I don't even recall how I started writing, I was so young."

Dear Reader:

SILHOUETTE DESIRE is an exciting new line of contemporary romances from Silhouette Books. During the past year, many Silhouette readers have written in telling us what other types of stories they'd like to read from Silhouette, and we've kept these comments and suggestions in mind in developing SILHOUETTE DESIRE.

DESIREs feature all of the elements you like to see in a romance, plus a more sensual, provocative story. So if you want to experience all the excitement, passion and joy of falling in love, then SILHOUETTE DESIRE is for you.

Karen Solem
Editor-in-Chief
Silhouette Books

NORA POWERS
In A Stranger's Arms

Silhouette Desire

Published by Silhouette Books New York

America's Publisher of Contemporary Romance

For another Emily

SILHOUETTE BOOKS, a Division of Simon & Schuster, Inc.
1230 Avenue of the Americas, New York, N.Y. 10020

Distributed by Pocket Books

ISBN: 0-671-47205-4

First Silhouette Books printing July, 1984

10 9 8 7 6 5 4 3 2 1

America's Publisher of Contemporary Romance

Printed in the U.S.A.

1

The Montana sun was warm, and out beyond the corral the range was still invitingly green. Emily Asperson wished she could be out there, enjoying a good gallop, instead of standing here rapidly getting nowhere. She stifled a sigh and looked up at the tall, dark, ruggedly handsome man beside her. Jerry Graves was very attractive. There was no doubt about that.

"I'd like to go to the dance with you," she told him again, trying to keep her voice patient. "But I'm competing tomorrow. I can't afford to be out so late. Brockway's fifty-five miles away, you know."

Absently she stroked the nose the chestnut mare thrust against her.

Jerry shrugged impatiently. "Of course, I know. I came off the circuit especially to take you to this dance."

Emily continued her stroking and kept a rein on her

temper. How like Jerry to expect her to drop all her plans the moment he arrived!

"I really am sorry," she said again. "But I just can't do it. You should have called me ahead. I've put up entry money, you know."

He ignored that. As she knew he would. Jerry thought woman's rodeo was a joke. A big joke.

"Then I guess I'll just have to take someone else," he said gruffly.

She held back another sigh. Even though Jordan, the closest town to the Double A Ranch, was over fifty miles from any other town, she knew Jerry wouldn't have any trouble finding someone. He attracted women like flies to honey. The trouble was—he knew it.

She tried for a light tone. "I guess you will. You won't have any trouble, I'm sure."

"Hell and damnation, Emily!" The words burst from him in a half shout that sent Gypsy skittering away from the fence. "When are you going to stop this silly playing at rodeo and act like a woman ought to?"

She lost the battle with her temper then. Maybe it was because she no longer had the mare's velvet-soft, comforting nose under her fingers. Whatever the reason, her patience had deserted her.

She whirled so quickly that her Stetson blew off her head and lay ignored in the dust. Her blue eyes blazing, she let him have it. "My rodeoing is just as important to me as yours is to you." She ignored his snort of derision, but it certainly didn't help to dampen her anger. "It's not my fault that the PRCA doesn't allow women to compete or that men like you don't take us seriously."

She took a deep breath and became vaguely aware

that another man, a stranger, was standing some distance behind Jerry, an expression of acute embarrassment on his face. Well, whoever he was, he was going to get an earful. She was tired of being taken for granted, of being patronized. Good and tired.

"Now you're being silly," Jerry said. "You know that you're my girl. I want you to be with me." Totally unaware that they had an audience, he reached out for her.

Emily evaded his hands, her anger growing. "Oh, no, you don't!" she cried. "Kissing me won't do you a bit of good. I'm not some brainless thing to be kissed into obeying you!"

Jerry's temper, never too well in check, blazed higher. "Sometimes I think you're not a woman at all," he shouted. "You sure don't act like one!" He jammed his Stetson down on his dark hair and growled, "I'm going to find me a real woman."

"Good luck!" she threw at him.

He whirled on his heel and caught sight of the stranger. For a second she thought the newcomer might be in for trouble. But then Jerry stomped on, threw himself into his pickup and roared away.

She retrieved her Stetson, took a deep breath and tried to let her anger go. To help herself do that she took a good look at the stranger, who seemed unsure whether to approach her or not. Her sense of humor asserted itself momentarily and she thought wryly that he must be wondering what kind of woman he was facing here.

He was tall, though not as tall as Jerry, and very lean. His blond hair was sun-streaked, his eyes a deep brown. His nose was strong and so was his chin, but he didn't have Jerry's half-sinister look, the look that she knew was so attractive to women.

She pushed the thought of Jerry from her mind and advanced toward the stranger. He was probably the student Dad had said was coming today.

"Hello," she said, forcing her voice into a welcoming tone. "I'm Emily Asperson and this is the Double A. Have you come about roping lessons?"

He took the hand she offered him. His handclasp was warm and firm, just as it should be, but his hand lacked calluses.

"My name is Alex Calloway," he replied. His voice was very rich, very deep. Strangely familiar in her ears, though she was sure she had never seen him before. "I was in touch with your father."

She nodded. "He told me. I'm sorry, we only hold our roping schools once a month and you just missed the last one."

Alex nodded. "Yes, I know. But he did say I could have some individual instruction."

She read hesitation in his face and before she could stop herself she snapped at him. "As long as you don't mind learning from a woman. Dad has other plans for this week."

A flicker of something crossed his face and vanished. She couldn't tell if it were amusement or surprise, but the deep voice remained neutral. "I have no objections to working with a woman," he said. "I also understand that you may be gone part of the time."

That was as close as he came to referring to the quarrel he had just overheard. She couldn't help appreciating his tact.

"I only have one rodeo this week," she said. "But I'll be gone the whole day."

He nodded. "Is that your horse?"

"Yes, that's Gypsy." She glanced to where the

chestnut was standing by the bars, calm now that the angered Jerry was gone. "She's a great roping horse."

The mare stuck an inquiring nose over the bars and Alex walked closer and rubbed it with an ease that spoke of long association with horses. "I don't know how much your father told you," he began.

Emily smiled at the mare's evident delight in finding a new friend. "Not very much. Just that you wanted special instruction."

He nodded. "Well, then, let me give you some background."

She knew already that he was an easterner. His accent gave him away, of course. His voice lacked the slow, drawling quality of western speech. And his clothes were too new. Oh, the jeans were weathered and the boots scuffed. But his Stetson had plainly not seen much wear. And his hands, long and slender, were too light and unscarred to belong to a cowman.

"I'm from Ohio," he said, shifting his gaze to her and continuing to rub the mare's nose.

"You've been around horses," she said quietly.

He nodded. "Yes, I know horses. You won't have to teach me to ride."

"Only to rope," she said. "You know," she went on, "most competitors are cowmen. They've been around stock all their lives, worked in the out-of-doors."

His smile was so disarming she almost lost her train of thought.

"I don't intend to compete," he said.

For a minute she didn't know what to say. "Then what are you doing here?"

"I'm a writer," he explained. "I'm doing a book on rodeo. I thought learning something about the events might help in the writing."

She nodded; then with another glance at his hands, she hurried on. "You aren't going to . . ." She stopped, aware that this was decidedly undiplomatic.

He laughed, a deep booming sound that again seemed so familiar, and that inexplicably made her feel happy. "Don't worry," he said. "I saw you looking at my hands. I know my limits, Miss Asperson. Let me assure you of that."

"Fine," she said.

He nodded. "I have no intention of contending with a bucking horse or a bull. Vicious beasts, I understand."

His dark eyes regarded her thoughtfully and she was aware of a funny kind of feeling in her stomach. To counteract it, she rushed into speech. "You mustn't believe everything you hear. Bucking stock is just that—bucking stock. Viciousness has nothing to do with it. Most bucking horses are tame pets—until you get on their backs."

"And the bulls?" he replied.

Emily laughed. "My brother Ted rides the bulls. It's true they try to stomp men sometimes. But Ted claims the bulls enjoy the competition as much as the men."

"How can they enjoy that kind of treatment? It seems inhumane."

There was something strange about his tone, but she ignored it as she rushed in to defend the rodeo. "That's silly. Rodeo animals lead good lives. Good bucking stock is expensive. And hard to find. Stock contractors can't afford to have their animals abused." She smiled, conscious that she'd been rattling on. "Why, most bucking stock live very long lives and are retired to green pastures."

"Well," he said, moving easily away from the subject, "as I was telling you, I don't intend to participate actively in the riding sports. I'm just going to see what kind of information I can pick up."

"What kind of book are you writing?" she asked.

That funny look crossed his face again. "Nonfiction. I haven't gotten the exact slant yet. But nonfiction. And about rodeo."

She opened her mouth, then closed it again. What on earth had she been thinking of? She couldn't go telling this stranger about their plans. She hadn't told anyone—not even her mother—about the plans she and the others had made at the beginning of the season. But the thought was always there, in the back of her mind, the thought of making men realize the unfairness of their actions, the stupidity of their macho rules.

"How long do you intend to stay here?" she asked, then felt a sudden embarrassment and hurried to add, "So I can arrange my schedule."

He gave her that charming smile again. "I'm figuring on about a week this time. Your father said I could use the Double A as a kind of home base for a while."

Emily chuckled. "Jordan's kind of far from everything," she pointed out.

"I know."

Something in his voice told her he was recalling her argument with Jerry. "I've been studying my map. But Jordan is sort of in the center of this half of the state."

She nodded. "Yes, that's true." She looked toward his blue Ford wagon—a durable older model.

He followed her gaze. "I'm used to doing a lot of driving," he said. "I've got the old boy fixed up with a tape recorder and mike. I do a lot of my writing while I'm traveling."

She smiled. "Looks like you're all set, then." She

glanced down at her watch. "Let me show you the bunkhouse and you can get settled in. We usually eat around six. You'll hear the dinner bell in time to wash up."

Together they went back to the car and she watched as he pulled out a battered bag.

"No typewriter?" she asked. "I always thought writers traveled around with those little portable typewriters."

His smile was friendly and warm. She liked the way his lips curved, the warmth in his eyes. Something about him made her feel good inside.

"Sorry to destroy the image," he said as he closed the tailgate, "but writers have been getting updated. When I'm at home, I do my writing on a personal computer. When I'm traveling, I send my tape cassettes back to a word processing office and they do it for me."

She shook her head. "Seems kind of complicated. I guess maybe I'm old-fashioned." She swept a glance around them. "Things haven't changed much around here for a long time. Did you stop in Jordan?" she asked as they moved off toward the weather-beaten bunkhouse.

"Yes. And I liked it. Are those the original false fronts on the buildings?"

Emily nodded. "Yes. Most of them are over seventy years old. The office building of the town's first doctor is there. He got here in 1916."

"The *first* doctor?" he repeated.

"Yes. He was the *only* doctor till about ten years ago." She laughed at his astonishment. "This is Montana, Mr. Calloway."

"Alex. Call me Alex," he corrected as they reached the bunkhouse.

She pushed open the door for him. "This is Montana, Alex. The Big Open, they call this region. Distances are big here. Ranches and towns few and far between." She smiled. "But we're used to it. We like it that way."

She made a gesture that included the empty room. "Twelve bunks. These six belong to the regular hands. These the students use. Take your pick." With a smile she indicated the old iron stove in the middle of the room. "Firewood's outside the door. Nights get chilly, even in summer. But the hands don't fire up unless it gets close to freezing. Your best bet's to grab a couple of extra blankets."

He nodded. "This is a rough life, isn't it?"

She had to pause, to consider his statement. Then she shrugged. "I suppose you could say that. I don't think of it that way. It's a good life. I wouldn't want any other."

He shoved his bag under one of the bunks and turned to her. "It's a long time till dinner, Miss Asperson."

"Emily," she corrected him. She always put herself on a first-name basis with the students. Usually, though, they were women. A western man wouldn't want a woman to teach him anything to do with rodeo.

"Emily," he said, and the deep, rich voice seemed to caress the word, sending a little shiver down her spine. Something stirred in her mind. She *knew* she had heard that voice before.

"I wonder," he went on, then hesitated as though debating with himself. Finally he gave her a boyish grin. "There's no use pretending I didn't hear what was going on between you and that cowboy."

15

She shrugged. "You could hardly help it. We weren't exactly quiet."

"The point is . . . I was wondering . . . Well, I've been driving all day. And the prairie looks so beautiful. I'd like to take a ride. Your father said there'd be a horse for me."

She nodded. "He probably told you, too, that you couldn't go wandering off alone. The prairie looks flat, but it can be deceptive. It's easy to get lost out there."

His grin had become more relaxed. "I can see that. So my problem is this: I want to go for a ride, but I guess you'd have to go with me. You seem to have been selected to ride herd on the tenderfoot. And I couldn't help overhearing that you're going to compete tomorrow. There must be things you have to do."

She liked this man. She liked him a lot. He was different from most of the men she knew. Her father and her brothers, Joe and Ted, were big, boisterous men. Her father gave his tacit support to her rodeoing, though she knew he wanted her to settle down and raise a family. But her brothers were more like Jerry. They thought rodeo was for men, and men only.

With a start she realized that the stranger was still staring at her. "Sorry, I was just thinking of what I have to do." She smiled and was pleased to see his answering smile. "And the first thing on my list is to give Gypsy some exercise. So let's get you a horse and a saddle. No reason you can't come along."

"Thank you," he said as he held the bunkhouse door open for her. "I appreciate this."

"It's just part of my job," she returned.

He didn't say anything to that and they approached the corral in friendly silence, pausing by the railing.

"You can have your pick of several horses," she said. "Most of the herd's on the range right now. Butcher Boy—he's the bay gelding over there—is apt to be a little touchy, takes a strong hand. The paint, Fancy Lady, will give you a good ride and no tricks. And Percival"—she indicated a big, rawboned gray— "might not look like much, but his gallop is as smooth as a rocking chair. In the arena, he still can't be beat. He's one of the best roping horses the rodeo's ever seen."

She turned to him with a little smile. "So which one will it be?"

He shook his head. "I don't know. I'll leave it up to you."

She considered. "Have you been riding regularly?"

"I have a gelding back in Ohio," he said. "I ride when I can."

She barely stopped herself from looking again at his hands. Could he handle a horse like Butcher Boy? But if she mounted him on one of the others, would he think she didn't believe him, didn't trust in his ability? For a minute she wondered why she was going through all this mental debate. Ordinarily the men that didn't bring their own mounts were just assigned one and that was that. She realized with something of a shock that she wanted this tenderfoot to think well of her, to like her. And she most certainly didn't want him to get hurt.

Stop arguing with yourself, she said internally. "Might as well take Butcher Boy," she told him and was rewarded by a quick flash of pleasure on his face. "He needs some exercise."

She led the way to the tack room, hoping that she hadn't made a mistake. "You take a lighter riding saddle." She indicated a row of them along one wall. "Bridle's over there. I'm going to use my roping saddle. Might practice on a few calves out there."

He nodded and turned to reach for a saddle. She took the opportunity to hoist down her own and moved toward the gate that led from the stable to the corral.

"I'll carry . . ." he began, but she was already there. Her bridle over her shoulder, her saddle resting against her boot, she whistled softly.

Gypsy came immediately and obediently offered her head for the bridle. Emily ground-tied the mare and slipped the saddle blanket over the smooth, rounded back. With a pat to the mare's flank, she bent to the saddle and barely avoided banging heads with Alex. His face was disturbingly close as he said, "I'll lift it."

She straightened. "There's no need. I wouldn't get far if I couldn't saddle my own horse."

"I know. But please, I still feel guilty about taking up your time."

She shrugged. "All right, then. Go ahead."

He swung the saddle up easily. She'd had no doubts about that. He pulled both the front cinch and back girth snugly tight, nudging the mare's belly to get her to release the air she had stored there, and stuck his hand up under the pommel to see that the blanket was lying right. She nodded approvingly. He knew his stuff. "Thank you."

"You're welcome."

She turned back to the corral, emitting another, deeper whistle. The bay trotted over and thrust his nose inquiringly into her hand.

"He's a beauty," Alex said, reaching out to stroke

the white patch that led down to the gelding's velvet-soft nose.

"Yes." She stood back and let Alex make friends with the horse. He seemed entirely at ease. After a few minutes, he bridled and saddled the gelding. She could find no fault with the process, none whatsoever.

She closed the gate between the corral and stable and walked Gypsy over to the one that opened into the ranch yard. "It's better to mount him outside the corral," she said. "He might want to do a little bucking. And don't let him run away with you out on the range. This is prairie dog country. And a broken leg means a horse has to be put down. Their legs are really rather fragile."

"I hear you," he said, leading the bay through the gate and waiting until she had mounted. Then he swung up with practiced ease, his hands just right on the reins. Butcher Boy pranced a little, lifting his hooves high, but he didn't attempt to buck.

Emily smiled in satisfaction—and relief. The horse knew that the man on his back was in control. Those lean hands were stronger than they looked.

"Now," she said, turning Gypsy toward the prairie, "let's have that ride."

2

Emily pushed her Stetson farther down on her short-cropped black curls and turned to the man beside her. He was good with the gelding, keeping him to a steady pace, though Butcher Boy was obviously eager to run. She liked the firm way Alex controlled the bay so that the horses walked side by side, and he and she were knee to knee.

He caught her glance and smiled. "This is beautiful country. I love the prairie. There's something special about it, I think. What did you say they call this region?"

"The Big Open," she replied. "The photographer L. A. Huffman called it that."

Alex frowned thoughtfully. "I've seen his stuff. The latter part of the 1800s, wasn't he? He did Indian portraits, among other things."

She nodded. "For an easterner you know a lot."

He shrugged. "I had a bad case of cowboy fever as a kid. I think my mother still has my six-gun tucked away someplace." He chuckled and glanced down at his scuffed boots. "I was wearing cowboy boots a long time before they were 'in.' When I grew up, I still loved the West."

His grin was engaging. "No more cowboy and Indian shoot-em-ups now. But the land's here." His hand went to the bay's arching neck and stroked the smooth muscles. "And the horses."

"But why Montana?" she asked. "There are other western states."

"I did a piece on Butte a while back," he said. "Anaconda and the dying copper mines. Since I was already out here, I took a little time for a vacation. Saw some of the rest of the state."

"So you've been in the mountains, too."

He nodded. "Yellowstone and Glacier." His expression turned thoughtful. "They're beautiful. Majestic and grand. But the prairie . . ." His face reflected the depth of his feeling. "Nothing can beat the prairie. It's so . . . so timeless."

She nodded. "I expect a lot of us take it for granted. I know I did until I went away to school."

"Where to?"

"Chicago."

"Whew!" He whistled. "That's quite a switch. And how did you like the Windy City?"

"I didn't mind the wind," she said, matching his grin with one of her own. "What I minded was the people. So many of them." A shudder of distaste shivered through her. "And nowhere to get away from them. Even in my room. And the noise . . . I don't know how people can stand it. Was I ever glad to get home."

She laughed softly. "The first thing I did was ride out here during what would be rush hour there and just sit, listening to the silence."

The sweet trill of bird song cascaded through the air. "And the meadowlarks," she said, gesturing toward the black-and-gold bird that was soaring skyward.

"What did you study in school?" he asked.

"Photojournalism." She didn't know why she was telling him this. She rarely spoke of personal things to the roping students.

He eyed her sharply. "And why did you quit?"

"I didn't. I'm not a quitter. I graduated." She smiled. "I even had a job. For a paper in one of the suburbs. But I couldn't handle city living. So I came home."

"And now?" he prompted.

"And now I teach roping to women students and I compete in women's rodeo."

"And your photography?"

"I take some pictures now and then. When I feel like it."

"Could I see some of them?"

"Maybe." She wondered again what had come over her. She never showed her photos to students. She never really got to know the people she worked with. About the only ones who appreciated her photos were her parents, and with them it was just affection. They really knew nothing about composition or any of the rest of it.

She didn't tell him, either, that someday she hoped to do a book of her own, a book about women in rodeo. For there had been rodeo women in the beginning—regular, ordinary women. Not psuedomen like Calamity Jane and her kind.

She pulled her mind back to the man beside her. "How did you get to be a writer?"

He shrugged, but his dark eyes twinkled. "I don't really know. Back in my younger days I used to write my own cowboy stories." He grinned again. "My heroes surpassed even Ned Buntline's in the magnitude of their deeds."

"You've read Ned Buntline, too?" she asked.

"Of course. I stumbled on a biography of him at a book sale. *The Great Rascal,* I think it was called. And appropriately so. The man was all that and more. Why, he made Buffalo Bill into a living legend."

"The power of the press," she said with a smile and he nodded.

The prairie was a vast carpet and myriad fragile wild flowers dotted its greenness as it stretched away into the horizon.

"I'd sure enjoy a good gallop," he said. "What do you do when you want a good run?"

"I'll show you." She nudged Gypsy into a trot and made toward a clump of cottonwoods clustered beside a small stream. "If you should ever get lost in prairie country," she said as they reined in beside the clear water, "you just look for the trees. Out here, trees mean water."

She wheeled her horse. "Now, look that way."

His gaze followed her extended hand. "Yes?"

"I scouted out this land just yesterday. No prairie dogs around. So we'll have our run in that direction." She gave him a serious glance. "Stay with me and pull up when I do. Okay?"

"Okay, boss." A grin accompanied the words, but she still wondered if she were coming on too strong.

She was used to instructing women students. And

they were used to taking orders, she thought with a touch of bitterness. Her father usually didn't give her the men, since they were likely to complain at the indignity of being taught by a woman. Well . . . She shook her thoughts free of that. He was her responsibility and she would treat him just like any other student. "Ready?" she asked.

"Ready," he replied.

So were the horses, she thought, as she clapped heels to Gypsy's sides and they took off. Her Stetson blew off her head and dangled by its thongs, bouncing on her back, even before Gypsy hit her full stride. And beside her, Butcher Boy was exultant, plainly enjoying this run for which he'd been itching.

As the ground flew beneath the horses' hooves, Emily let the glory of the ride sweep her up. There was nothing, nothing in this whole world, as wonderful as galloping across this great green expanse, with the wind in her hair and Gypsy's perfect body moving beneath her.

Far too soon it was time to call a halt and as she eased the mare down to a walk, she glanced over to see how Alex was doing with the bay. It was clear that Butcher Boy would have liked to keep running, but he was obeying the hands on his reins. They might be pale and unscarred, those hands, but they were strong.

"That was great," Alex said as they turned their horses and began the walk back toward the stream. "I haven't had such a good run in years."

Emily nodded. "There's just something about a good gallop. It blows the cobwebs out of your mind." She smiled sheepishly. "I think I read that somewhere."

"Whoever said it hit the nail on the head," he

replied. "I feel really fresh now. No more highway fatigue."

"It's a long stretch from Brockway," she agreed. "But the prairie is beautiful."

He nodded. "Yes. And I'm used to driving. But tell me, how did you come to compete in rodeo?"

"It's a long story."

He shrugged. "It's not exactly like I was racing to catch a plane."

She had to laugh at that, knowing that no planes, trains or even buses stopped at Jordan, and knowing that Alex knew it, too.

"Okay," she began. "Just remember. You asked for it."

"I'm all ears."

"My dad's rodeo. He was champion calf roper a couple of times. All-round cowboy once. He rode bulls when he was real young. When he came back from Korea, he gave up the bulls and just roped. He *says* Mom made him quit. He met her there. In Korea. She was a nurse. But I think quitting was just as much his idea." She grinned. "No one ever *made* my dad do anything. Besides, I heard him say one day that he'd used up all his luck over there and he couldn't afford to give the bulls any more chances."

Alex nodded gravely. "Go on."

"So Dad came home and brought Mom with him. She was from New York. He competed in the roping events and they took over the ranch. It had been his father's. They raised horses and a few years ago Dad opened the roping school."

"Do you have brothers and sisters?" Alex asked.

"No sisters. Two brothers." She grimaced. "They're kind of like Jerry. Same attitude. They're on the road now."

"Do they rope?"

"No. They both know how, and they're pretty good at it, but they like the contact stuff better. Joe junior rides the saddle broncs. Ted rides the bulls."

"I see. So you're the only roper."

She nodded. "Yep. Dad says he found me roping fence posts when I was five and took me in hand."

Alex laughed. She liked his laugh. It was warm and . . . She couldn't think of the right word to describe the good feeling it gave her. "Comfortable" seemed almost right, but that was an odd word to use in regard to a stranger.

"So now I compete. In women's rodeo, of course. The men won't let us compete with them."

The bitterness in her voice bewildered him. She could see it in his face. "I don't understand," he said. "What do you mean?"

"The only event in standard rodeo open to women is barrel racing. And that depends mostly on the horse." She wondered how she'd gotten started like this, but somehow she couldn't seem to stop. "Women can perform every bit as well as men, whether it's roping calves or riding bulls."

"But why should they want to?" he asked, so quietly that she couldn't take offense.

"For one thing PRCA rodeos have much bigger purses. And then there's prestige. And the challenge."

He nodded. "I can understand that. And your need for recognition. But if rodeo is a sport—that's what they say, isn't it?"

She nodded.

"Well, if rodeo is a sport like other sports, then where's your precedent? Football, baseball, basketball, boxing, hockey, skiing, swimming, diving, tennis.

Men and women don't compete against each other in any of them."

"That doesn't make it right."

"Of course not." His voice was soothing. "I'm not taking sides. I'm trying to understand."

"So, go on," she said, surprised at herself. But she did believe what he said. He was trying to understand.

"So, maybe it would be to your advantage to try to make women's rodeo stronger. Like tennis and swimming. They've become very good sports for women."

She shook her head. "There are some precedents. Show jumping competitions are mixed. And racetracks allow women jockeys now."

He looked thoughtful. "That's true."

"Both of those have horses in them, too."

He nodded. "Actually, some people would say that in those cases it's the horse that's actually competing."

Emily's snort of derision made the mare's ears quiver. "And you think that isn't true in rodeo? A good horse makes all the difference in the world to a roper. And in the riding events . . ." She stroked the mare's neck as they ambled on. "In the riding events the animal's so important that it gets a score, too. The higher the animal's rank, the higher the score."

Alex nodded. "I can see you've given this a lot of thought."

She laughed. The bay skittered nervously, but Alex kept him in hand.

"All my life my brothers have been putting me down. I can't do this. I shouldn't do that. And all because I'm female." She scowled. "They used to pick on me a lot when I was little. You know how big brothers are."

He nodded, waiting silently for her to go on.

"One day, Mom saw them."

"I bet they got it then."

Emily shook her head. "Mom's smarter than that. She took me aside and taught me how to defend myself." She saw the disbelief in his eyes and she laughed. "I'm little, huh? And my brothers each top six feet."

"How could you—" he began.

"How could I defend myself?"

"Yes."

"Mom was an army nurse. They taught her karate. She taught me on the sly, when no one was around. Then one day Joe messed with me and ended up in the dirt." She laughed, this time with genuine merriment. "I'll never forget the surprised look on his face. Teddy didn't believe it when he heard. He had to get thrown, too. After that they both treated me with more respect."

He raised an eyebrow. "I imagine so."

"Anyhow," she said, tracing her thoughts backward to what she'd started to say. "I'm as good as any man at calf roping. But because I'm a woman I get hardly anything for it. That's not right."

He nodded. "I take it from what you say that the men out here don't think much of women rodeoing."

"You take it right," she said. "They want all the glory for themselves." She sniffed. "Women are supposed to be soft and feminine. Waiting around for their men to come home." She gave him a withering glance. "Like Jerry. He comes into town and expects me to drop everything to go to a dance with him." She felt her lips drawing into a thin line. "It's like I don't exist until he wants me. Like I'm just sitting on a shelf waiting. I hate it!"

"Men are not the only ones who behave that way," he said softly. "There are some women like that, too."

"Well, good for them," she snapped, and instantly regretted it. "No, I don't mean that. It isn't going to make things any better if women start behaving as stupidly as men have."

"Present company excepted, of course," he said with just the beginning of a grin.

He took her by surprise with these words and a little giggle burst from her lips. "Oh, of course."

"Now," he said, his face gone serious again. "I've a few more questions I'd like to ask. Just playing devil's advocate, you understand."

She was smiling now. It was hard to stay angry with Alex. Silly, too. After all, none of this was his fault. "Ask away."

"I understand about the calf roping, but what about the contact stuff? Riding the broncs and the bulls? Isn't that dangerous?"

She shrugged. "I suppose so. It's dangerous for the men, too. So what? Women aren't children. They don't need protection. Women do all sorts of dangerous things and nobody stops them. They skydive." She grinned. "Now I call that really dangerous. A horse's back is as far off the ground as I want to get. The point isn't whether something is dangerous or not," she went on. "The *point* is that women shouldn't be excluded because of their sex."

"You talk a great argument," he said. "I'm convinced."

She laughed. "It's nice of you to say so, anyhow. And to listen to me talk. After all, you're supposed to be learning about roping."

He shrugged and she noticed for the first time the

breadth of the shoulders under the faded plaid shirt. He was leaner than her brothers, but he was a well-built man. "There's plenty of time for that," he said. "I'd like to learn everything I can about the rodeo. The more I know the better. So, if you don't mind, I'll be asking all kinds of questions."

"I'll be glad to answer them," she replied. "If I can. But you'll probably want to go behind the chutes at a couple of rodeos. You can hear a lot back there." She tried to keep the anger out of her voice, but she wasn't quite successful. "Women aren't allowed back there."

He looked rather surprised. "Why not?"

"The official word is that we might get hurt." She snorted. "We've been around stock just as much as the men. They just like to keep it their private preserve."

"What about women's rodeo?" he asked. "Do you allow men behind the chutes?"

Her laughter was strained. "I'll say we do. We also have male officials."

They had reached the clump of cottonwoods by now and Gypsy stopped obediently. Emily found that she wanted to forget about the rodeo. It was old irritation. There was no point in letting it spoil the afternoon. She swung down from the saddle. "Let's give the horses a drink and rest a little."

"Sure," Alex answered, also swinging down. "I haven't been doing much riding lately," he said with a slight smile. "My legs will appreciate a rest. To say nothing of another part of me."

They stood silent as the horses drank. Then Emily turned back toward a big cottonwood. "Want to sit awhile?"

Alex laughed. "I may not want to *sit* for several

days, but I'd like to stretch out. Where shall we leave the horses?"

She dropped Gypsy's reins by a patch of buffalo grass. "This looks good."

He eyed her a minute. "This horse is going to stay here if I drop his reins?"

"Sure. He's a western horse. He's been well trained. When his reins are hanging, he's ground-tied. A cowboy can't risk having his horse run off. It's a long walk back to the ranch house." She smiled. "And one thing you learn quick out here—a cowboy without his horse is in bad, bad shape. Cowboys really hate being afoot."

They had reached the tree and she settled herself under it. Alex stretched out beside her, his head resting on his hands. "Have you had Gypsy long?" he asked.

Emily looked at the chestnut peacefully cropping grass and smiled. "Dad raised her. Trained her specially for me. She's a beautiful performer."

She leaned back against the tree trunk and smiled at him. "I don't know where they got the idea that a dog is man's best friend. I think that position belongs to the horse.

"Take a good roping horse now, a horse like Gypsy. The horse has to rate the speed of the calf, stop when you want it to, then back off to keep the rope taut while you run down the rope to tie the calf. The horse makes the difference every time. Someone has said that a good horse counts for about seventy-five percent." She shook her head. "The horse can't do it all, of course. He can't throw the rope or tie the calf, but he can get you in the right spot to throw and he can hold the rope taut till you run down it and make the tie."

He nodded. "Isn't all that quick stopping hard on the horse?" he asked, lying on his back and looking up at the sky.

"I wear skid boots on Gypsy to protect her fetlocks."

"I suppose you'll have to start training a replacement soon," he continued idly.

Emily looked at him in surprise. "Whatever for? Good rodeo horses work into their twenties. Even good bucking horses."

His head turned quickly. "Are you telling me that those wild rides don't hurt the animals?"

She laughed. "Rodeo animals are among the best cared-for in the world. A good bucking horse brings in the money. For stockman and rider both. A lot of them seem to enjoy the competition. Like the bulls. Only friendlier."

"I see." He closed his eyes and she couldn't resist the temptation of studying his face. It was a strong face, with good clean lines, a bold nose and a firm jaw. Not spectacularly handsome, yet very attractive.

He opened his eyes suddenly and caught her looking at him. To her dismay she felt the blood rushing to her cheeks. To cover her confusion, she glanced at her watch. "Guess we'd better be heading back. I've some other things to do."

"Of course." He was on his feet instantly, smiling down at her and extending a hand to help her up. There was no way to avoid seeing that hand; it was right in front of her face. Yet she was strangely reluctant to take it.

She put her hand in his, feeling the warmth, the strength of his fingers. He gave a tug, pulling her upright.

She meant to disengage her fingers the moment she

reached her feet, but somehow her boot caught on a clump of grass or a root, and she lost her balance and staggered. The next thing she knew she was up against his chest. Her free hand had come up to help with her balance and it went automatically to his shoulder as his arms encircled her.

For an instant frozen in time she stood there, her body pressed against his, while incredible feelings raced through her.

And then the moment was gone. His arms fell away and she moved back. "Are you all right?" he asked.

"Yes, yes." She didn't dare raise her eyes to his. What if he could see something in them, what if he could read there the feelings that had almost overwhelmed her during those brief moments in his arms?

She turned back toward the horses. "You'll want to wash up before dinner."

3

When Emily woke up the next morning, it was with a smile, in spite of the fact that it was still dark outside. The all-girl rodeo she meant to compete in was some distance away. As she quickly showered and pulled on her clothes, she whistled noiselessly through her teeth. She had forced herself to relax and sleep the night before, even though her mind kept wanting to replay the events of the afternoon.

Now, pulling on her boots, she recalled again that intense moment in Alex's arms. Neither of them had referred to it afterward and once they were on their way back to the ranch, he had begun to ask more questions about rodeoing.

Gradually her embarrassment over the incident had faded, so that by the time they neared the ranch house she was feeling more comfortable again. And then Alex had asked, "Where are you competing tomorrow?"

"At Browning," she had answered.

"Is your family going along to watch?"

Emily shook her head. "No. It's too far and Dad's too busy."

He looked like he was about to ask her something more, then changed his mind. "I see. Got a friend going along?"

Emily shook her head again. "Not this trip. Cherry's been competing over near Glacier. We'll meet at Browning."

"And who is Cherry?"

"She's my heeler. In team roping," she explained. "I rope the calf's head. She gets the heels."

He nodded. "I see. Well . . . if you're going alone . . . that is . . . I'd like to see the rodeo." He sounded almost embarrassed. "I'd like to go along."

"It's only women, you know." She tried to ignore a feeling of joy.

"I know. But if you're in it, I know I'll enjoy watching."

He really had said that, she reminded herself. She finished pulling on her other boot and threw a quick glance at the clock. He hadn't batted an eye when she'd told him to be ready at 5 A.M. either.

She grabbed up her bag and tiptoed down the stairs to the kitchen. It took only a few minutes to boil water for a Thermos of coffee and pick up the sack of sweet rolls her mother had baked. They could eat while they were driving.

She put the food in the front seat of the car and tossed her bag in the back. Alex's battered bag was already there and she caught herself smiling.

She checked the trailer hitch one more time, then went into the stable to get Gypsy. Her tack and gear were already loaded; she always did all she could the night before to save time.

As she entered the stable, Alex turned from the stall where he'd been leaning, admiring her father's paint horse. "Good morning," he said, in that deep, melodious voice.

"Good morning, Alex. Did you sleep well?"

He chuckled. "Yes. But it's lucky I took your advice and put some extra blankets handy. It gets cold here at night."

"That it does. Coffee and rolls in the car." She caught his eye and smiled. "It's a piece to the next town. We can eat while we're traveling."

"Sure. I'm all ready. Anything I can do to help?"

She shook her head. "No. I just have to load Gypsy. I took care of everything else last night." She reached for the mare's halter and led her out of the stall. "I'll be ready to roll in a minute."

It was actually about five minutes later when she climbed in the car and settled herself behind the wheel.

"You drive this rig yourself?" Alex asked as they drove down the lane, leaving the still dark ranch house behind them.

She laughed. "Of course. One thing a woman learns early out here. If you want to compete, you've got to be able to do all that a man can do. And that means taking care of your own gear and driving your own rig."

He frowned. "Is that why the men don't like you competing? They think it's unfeminine?"

She shrugged. "It's hard to tell what men think. They're always talking about our hurting ourselves. Saying that we don't know how to handle animals."

Her laugh was just a little brittle. She didn't like the sound of it. "That's a crock of you-know-what," she went on. "I've been around stock all my life. Played under the horses' bellies. Been roping calves since I was eight. I'm only five feet five, but I can do anything with a rope that a man can. I can tie a calf just as well. And just as quick."

She snapped her mouth shut. There was that harsh note in her voice again. She didn't much like the sound of it. Besides, if she didn't get off this subject, she was apt to find herself telling him about their plan. And it was not her secret to tell.

"But what about the bucking events and steer wrestling?" he asked.

She managed a small smile and a calmer voice. "I've seen a little bit of a woman—only five feet tall—ride the broncs and the bulls. You don't need a lot of weight. What you need are strong arms. And guts."

Alex laughed at that, but he wasn't the kind of person to be distracted from his point. "And the steer wrestling?"

"I'll admit that's harder. But it's partly a question of leverage. I use some of the karate things I learned from Mom when I throw a calf. After all, a steer weighs a lot more than a man, too."

Alex chuckled. "You've got a point there all right. Still, it seems dangerous to me."

She gave him a little smile. "Living is dangerous," she said. "But it's the best we've got. Now"—she indicated the Thermos—"how about pouring us some coffee and breaking out the rolls?" She laughed suddenly, realizing how Jerry or her brothers would have responded to a request like that. But then, they would never have been going with her like this. "That is," she added, "if you don't mind doing women's work."

He chuckled with her. "No, I don't mind. It's the least I can do, since you're driving. Besides"—his voice grew serious—"I don't believe that jobs should be delegated like that—on the basis of sex. I think it might be very good for men if women were treated more as equals. It's a pretty insecure man who has to protect his own 'place' by keeping a woman in hers. Here you go."

She chanced a quick look at him as she took the proffered cup of coffee. His face was just as serious as his voice. She sipped tentatively, enjoying the warmth, before she asked, "Are there many men like you in Ohio? I sure didn't meet any in Chicago."

He laughed then. "Better not base any assumptions on me," he said. "I'm not a good sample."

"Oh? Why not?"

He had just bitten into a roll and he took his time chewing before he spoke. "Well, for one thing, I grew up without much male companionship. At least, the real kind. My dad never came back from Korea. My mother had to make it alone. She was a newspaperwoman before she married. Went back to it when Dad died. But there were five of us. The four girls and me." His smile was tight. "I was the oldest, you see. So I hung up my spurs to ride herd on the girls while Mom worked."

"Where are they now?" she asked, intrigued by this glimpse into his past.

"All grown up," he replied. "One's a doctor, one's a lawyer, one's a research chemist. And the baby— Becca—she's a novelist."

"Whew! You must have had quite a mother!"

Alex nodded thoughtfully. "She's a great person. A wonderful woman." He gave her a sidelong glance. "You'd like her. She's fiercely independent." He chewed thoughtfully. "She insisted that we all go to college. Said the girls could marry if they wanted to, but first they had to have careers."

"Did they marry?"

"Yes, all of them." He grinned. "They've made me an uncle a couple of times already."

"And you?" The words were out before she realized their import. She felt herself flushing. Alex's marital status wasn't any of her business. Nevertheless her fingers tightened on the wheel as she waited for his answer.

"Me? I'm still single." He laughed. "I don't quite know how it happened. Of course, I was pretty busy during high school, keeping the girls in line."

"Didn't you resent that?"

He turned to face her. "I might have. Except I saw how hard my mother worked. For us. So we could have a future. They didn't have much except us kids when Dad enlisted. Just five kids and a mortgaged house. But we managed. We had a lot of love." His voice grew wistful. "I guess I haven't married yet because I haven't found a girl like Mom."

He took another roll from the bag and laughed. "Besides, I raised four kids while Mom was on assignments. I know what it's like. How can I ask a woman to do that?"

He was laughing still, but even with her eyes on the road she sensed the underlying pain. He had lost those carefree adolescent days. He had sacrificed them willingly, it was true; but he had lost them, nevertheless, and the loss still had the power to hurt him.

"Well," she said, trying for a light tone. "I suppose if she loved you enough, it wouldn't be so hard. Women do that kind of thing all the time. My mom left all her family in New York to come west with Dad. Jordan is a lot different from New York City."

"Does she ever seem to mind?" Alex asked.

To her surprise, Emily had to stop to consider this. "I don't really know," she admitted at last. "She doesn't act like it."

Alex nodded and silence fell over them as they finished up the rolls. She kept her eyes on the road, but her mind was busy. Why had she never thought of her mother's move in these terms before? Just because she herself loved the vast land she'd been born and bred in, didn't mean that everyone did. What if her mother had found the West as difficult to adjust to as *she* had found Chicago? It was certainly a disquieting thought and one her mind would insist on reverting to for many days thereafter.

It was close to noon when they pulled in to Browning. Alex, stretching his legs outside the car, shook his head. "You're going to compete after a drive like that?"

She laughed. "Of course. We've got a couple of hours yet. Just let me get Gypsy settled and we'll walk around a bit."

The chestnut mare backed willingly out of the trailer and placidly followed Emily into the stall.

Alex tagged along, his eyes always busy. "She's very well behaved, isn't she."

Emily nodded. "Yes. Gypsy knows her business. Of course, there are bucking horses just as tame as this."

Alex pushed his Stetson to the back of his head. "Are you putting me on?"

"No. It's true. Like I told you. Bucking horses don't hate people. They just hate being ridden. Most of them are tame as anything. Easily transported."

Alex frowned thoughtfully. "I really thought they fought all the time."

She closed the stall door behind Gypsy and shook her head. "It's a good thing you came out here to see for yourself. You've got a lot of wrong ideas about rodeo."

A strange look crossed his face and vanished. "It's beginning to look that way," he mused. "It's really beginning to look that way."

"Hey, Em!" The cheerful call came from farther down the row of stalls.

Emily turned to meet the bouncy young woman with the brilliant red curls who came almost running up to them. "Hi, Cherry. When did you get in?"

"Made it last night. Petunia needed a good night's rest." Her laughter was infectious. "But not as much as I did." Her green eyes rested curiously on Alex. "Got a new friend?"

Emily smiled. "This is Alex Calloway. He's doing a book on rodeo. Came out to the Double A to learn about roping."

"Oh." A speculative look appeared in Cherry's eyes and Emily suppressed a sigh. She knew she would be bombarded with questions as soon as she and Cherry were alone.

"How do you like Montana, Mr. Calloway?"

Alex smiled. "Please, call me Alex. I like Montana just fine. It's great country." He stretched. "And big. Very big."

Both Cherry and Emily laughed. "It gets even bigger when you're hauling the old horse trailer across it," they chorused.

Emily turned to her friend. "We're just going to walk around a little, then get a cup of coffee."

"Sure. See you later."

For a minute Emily thought Cherry was going to suggest coming along. That would have been all right, but . . . She let the thought take shape: . . . but it was nicer to be alone with Alex. That didn't mean anything, though, she hastened to tell herself. She just enjoyed his company.

And who wouldn't? He was a man you could hold a decent conversation with. A man who could be a friend as well as a . . . She stopped that thought. Or tried to. It was too soon to think of things like that. Yet for a moment she was lost in the feeling of that second she had stood with his arms around her, and the intensity of the emotions that had threatened to swamp her then.

Suddenly she was conscious of his fingers under her elbow. "Which way?" he asked. "That Thermos of coffee is only a sad memory now. My stomach is demanding more."

She flashed him a smile. "Of course. This way."

As they made their way toward a refreshment stand, Alex looked around curiously. "Where are all the men?" he asked.

Emily shrugged. "Not many men bother with women's rodeo. They say it's too tame for them." She made an expressive face. "Most of the men you see here are working as officials or are here with some contestant as a kind of trainer-coach. My dad came along at first to watch me compete and make suggestions."

"Doesn't he come anymore?"

She shook her head. "The ranch takes a lot of time. The school, too."

"Does he go to see your brothers?"

"If they get up in the big-money stuff. We usually all go to the Cheyenne Frontier Days together." Her eyes began to gleam. "Now there's a rodeo. The best in the country. To compete there you have to have a lot of points."

"Points?"

"A cowboy gets one point for every dollar he earns in a PRCA-approved rodeo. The man with the most points wins. He's the champion whatever for the year. The all-round champion is the cowboy with the most points in two events."

"So it's not just a matter of skill," Alex said thoughtfully. "There's endurance to be considered. Obviously a man has to compete as much as possible to amass enough points."

Emily nodded. "Now someone really good can even go beyond the National Finals Rodeo."

"To become a movie star?" asked Alex with a grin.

Emily chuckled. "That's been done, too. But I'm talking about something else. The Rodeo Super Stars Competition. It was held in Fort Worth this last April. The top-ranked competitors from calf roping, barrel racing, bull riding and bareback bronc riding came together by invitation only. The top sixteen from each event, according to the PRCA's records. This contest is run differently from regular rodeos."

"How?" Alex was listening attentively. She realized how much she liked that, liked having a man pay real attention to what she was saying.

"This is a head-to-head event. Each contestant competes with the others. The fastest time or best score moves the contender into the next round. This past year, the winner in the calf roping collected twenty-five thousand dollars."

"Whew!" Alex whistled under his breath. "No wonder the rodeo attracts a lot of men."

"That sounds like big money," Emily went on. "And it is. But most cowboys don't earn anywhere near that. It costs money to rodeo, you know. We haul our own horses around the country. That takes money. We have to eat and sleep. And we have to put up entry money in order to get into an event. It's not exactly an easy way to get rich."

Alex's smile was amused. "I guess not." He looked thoughtful again. "Hospital bills must amount to a pretty penny, too."

Emily nodded. "They do for some. Ropers don't get hurt as often as the bucking riders and wrestlers, but there's always the chance."

"Stock must get hurt a lot, too."

There was a peculiar note in his voice, but his face didn't register any change in expression.

"Not like the men," Emily said. "Once in a while an animal falls and gets injured. But not often. They're too well protected. Good stock has a lot of money in it. Stockmen do their darnedest to protect their investments."

Alex was silent for a moment. "I guess that makes sense."

They had reached the lunch stand and he turned to her. "Lunch is on me. After all, you furnished breakfast."

"Okay, but mine'll have to be light. Too much food can sit like a lead weight in the stomach."

"Right."

As it turned out, they couldn't have gotten a full meal anyhow. Alex got hamburgers, fries and coffee for two and she followed him to a grassy spot under a tree.

For a little while they were too busy eating to talk. With his first hamburger under his belt, Alex smiled. "That feels better. So, let me see if I know what to look out for."

Emily nodded, noticing again how warm his dark-brown eyes could be.

"First off," he said, "you've got to be careful coming out. If the horse breaks the barrier, it means a ten-second penalty."

She nodded.

"Then you rope the calf as quick as you can. Gypsy slides to a halt and holds the rope taut while you dismount, run down it, flip the calf and tie three legs together. Then you raise your hands."

"Very good," said Emily.

"It almost takes longer to describe than to do," he said. "But how do you flip the calf?" His eyes traveled over her slender form and she felt herself growing warm inside and wondering if he liked what he saw. "I mean, I know you're strong," he went on. "But you're so . . ."

"Little?" she suggested.

"Yes," he said slowly. "But that isn't what I was going to say." He raised a hand as though to protect himself. "Now don't get mad at me." He was grinning, but he sounded half-serious. "It's just that you look so . . . so feminine."

"I do?" She considered this with some surprise. She had always associated femininity with ruffles and full skirts and long, flowing hair. Though she liked to get prettied up as much as the next girl, her everyday outfit, the inevitable jeans, plaid shirt and boots, certainly didn't seem feminine to her. Nor her short unruly curls. She shrugged. "What makes you say that?" she asked, more out of curiosity than anything else, though she was aware that his words were very pleasing to her.

"I . . ." He hesitated. "I don't really know," he conceded at last. "There's just something so womanly about you."

He gazed so long into her eyes after he said this that she grew embarrassed and made a pretense of choking on a French fry so she could break contact with those disturbing eyes.

"I use the leverage things I learned in karate," she said when she quit coughing. "They work real good."

"Why don't you train the horse to throw the calf down?" he asked. "Wouldn't that make it easier?"

She shook her head. "I suppose it might. But it's not allowed. There has to be daylight under the calf when you get to it. That's the rule."

"So then you throw it?"

She nodded. "Yes."

"Explain to me about the tying."

"I'll teach you all this later," she said, munching the last of her French fries.

"That's good, I want to learn. But I want to understand what's going on today."

"Okay. I've got the piggin' string in my teeth, see. It's already got a loop in it. I jump off the horse—on the right side—run down the rope, throw the calf, hook the loop over one front foot, cross and tie two others. Then I throw up my hands and wait to see if the tie holds."

"I don't suppose the calf enjoys this much."

She gave him a strange look. He seemed awfully concerned about the animals. "I don't know. It doesn't seem to hurt them. Contestants can get fined, even disqualified, for letting the horse drag a calf. The slides on the lariats have to be tied with string, no metal on them at all. And calves don't stay in rodeo long. For women's rodeo they have to weigh under two hundred and twenty pounds. For men's they can go up to three hundred and fifty."

"Because men are stronger?" he asked, with a little gleam in his eyes.

"Because they *think* they are," she replied, wondering how she could possibly be laughing like this over something that had angered her for as long as she could remember.

"So what's a reasonably good time to do all that?" he asked.

"Twelve seconds is good. Usually good enough for day money. Though it's been done in less than nine. But there are so many things that can go wrong. If the horse breaks the barrier, that means a ten-second penalty. You can miss your first loop, lose your piggin' string. We have extras of each of those," she went on. "But it takes time to shake out a new loop. And time is what we don't have."

"You get off the right side of the horse? Isn't that dangerous?"

"Not when you have a well-trained horse. You just can't do it without the right kind of horse."

He nodded. "Yes, I'm seeing that clearer and clearer." He finished the last of his coffee. "Can I come back to the chutes with you?" he asked. "I'd like to see what it's like back there."

"I don't see why not. I've got a companion pass." She gave him what she hoped was a pleasant smile. "We don't keep people out."

He raised his hand again as though to defend himself. "You make me almost sorry to be a man," he said. And then that rich, melodious voice deepened even more as he leaned toward her, adding softly,

"But only in some ways. In other ways I couldn't be gladder."

His eyes, which were very close to hers, darkened, and she found that her heart was pounding in her chest as his gaze held hers fast.

A sharp snap brought her back to reality, and, looking down, she saw that she had inadvertently crushed her Styrofoam coffee cup, which now lay in two pieces in her hand.

"You *are* strong," he said, his voice returning to normal. "I'd better be careful not to cross you."

She saw the laughter in his eyes and she laughed with him. But she had also seen something more in those dark eyes. Alex Calloway knew that he had an effect on her, that she was attracted to him. And she wasn't sure whether to be glad or sorry that he knew.

4

~~~~~~~~~~~~~~~~~~~~

Later, behind the chutes as she readied Gypsy for their first go-round, Emily tried not to think of that breathless moment when their eyes had locked with such intensity. A rodeo competitor couldn't afford distractions like that.

But it was pretty hard to put Alex out of her mind when he was right there beside her, asking questions about this or that piece of Gypsy's equipment. And when she had answered all that, it was even worse. For the girls came then, all wanting introductions to this attractive newcomer.

She performed them, of course, but she was dismayed at the black feelings that struck her when she saw Alex surrounded by friendly, chattering girls. Black feelings of . . . jealousy.

She found it hard to believe. She would like very much for it not to be true. But she had never been very good at deceiving herself. So she had to admit that it *was* true. She was jealous, very jealous, about the stranger in whose arms she had rested for one brief, intense moment. She could not really say why. Perhaps it was because in the arms of this stranger, she had known an intensity of feeling that she had never experienced before.

He was, after all, very different from the men she had grown up with. Softer-voiced, more introspective, better able to understand a woman's feelings.

She crouched and inspected Gypsy's skid boots. She had already run over her equipment checklist. But right at the moment she didn't want to meet the eyes of the man who seemed to understand her feelings so well. She certainly didn't want him to know about this jealousy. As her fingers fiddled with the buckles, she tried to understand what was happening to her.

She'd been seeing Jerry Graves for over a year now—Jerry Graves, with his macho good looks. Whenever he took her out, even in Jordan, which wasn't exactly a big town, some woman would inevitably approach him in the course of the evening with a look in her eyes that was definitely predatory.

And she, Emily, had taken it all in her stride. Jealousy had been nothing but a word to her then. And now, now she was so jealous of this man that she hadn't even wanted her best friend to eat with them. She was being ridiculous. She'd had boyfriends in Chicago, men she liked, even admired. Several she had briefly considered marrying. But none of them had affected her as this man did, this stranger in whose arms she was overcome with such deep feelings.

She got to her feet. She could hardly stay crouched down there any longer.

"So," Alex said cheerfully from the other side of the mare. "All set?"

She nodded, swallowing over the lump in her throat. "Yes."

He ran a hand appreciatively over Gypsy's shining rump. "Now, let me see if I've got everything right." He looked down. "Those are skid boots on her back legs. To protect her fetlocks when she slides to a stop."

Emily nodded. "Right."

"This thing going down from her bridle is a tie-down. It keeps her from throwing her head back. Into your face or into the rope. This train chain goes on over the bridle. The rope threads through this ring and up to the saddle pommel. That keeps her from getting hurt by the rope and it also keeps her facing the calf."

He looked at her quizzically. "How'm I doing so far, teach?" he asked.

Emily found herself smiling. "So far you get an A plus."

"Now for the saddle," he said, his eyes meeting hers briefly across the horse's back, causing a catch in her breath that was almost audible.

"It's held in place by this wide breast collar, a front girth and a rear cinch. Two thick pads keep it from hurting her back."

He grinned at her as he stuck his fingers between the pommel and the pads. "This I didn't learn from you. If you can't get your fingers in here, it means the saddle's going to rub on her withers and make them sore."

"Right again," she said.

His smile was so warm she felt her whole body go hot. She had to stop this, she told herself silently. She couldn't afford to be thinking like this. Not now, when she had to compete.

"Spare lariat," he said, patting the spot where it

hung on the pommel. "Extra piggin' string in your back pocket. Anything else?"

"In another arena Gypsy might need splint boots to protect her splint bones. If the ground is real deep and she needs to push off to run, I'll put bell boots on her front legs."

Alex laughed and that feeling of warmth enveloped her. "The horse is certainly taken care of," he said. "Now where's all your protective equipment?"

She laughed, too. "I don't wear any. But then, I don't have to slide to a stop like she does. And when ropes are flicking around, I'm the one in control of them."

He nodded. "What kind of injuries are ropers apt to get?"

The question startled her and she wasn't fast enough to keep her reaction from showing on her face. "Well, we have to be careful with the rope. Got to keep the horn knot tight. A thumb caught between the loop and the saddle horn can be lost."

She saw the flicker of dismay in his eyes before they dropped to where her hand rested on the saddle. "Experienced ropers are careful," she told him. "And I still have both my thumbs." She extended her hands. "See?"

He grinned then, a grin to match hers. "Is that the only kind of accident you're prone to?"

She shrugged. "A person can fall dismounting. It's always possible to catch a foot in a stirrup getting off. That's embarrassing more than hurtful, usually. I suppose you could get kicked by the calf while you're tying it. Generally speaking, though, calf roping is one of the safest rodeo events. Men compete in it much longer than in the riding events. Often into their forties and fifties. Riders usually retire by the time they're thirty. Or earlier, if they get smashed up too bad."

"So the riders can really get hurt?"

She nodded. "A bronc or a bull rider who gets through an entire season without an injury is a rarity. Most of them get hurt at least once. Busted arms, legs, ribs. Those things aren't so bad. It's the head and back things that can really wipe a man out. Ruin his career for good."

She sighed. "If he's smart, a man'll get out while he's still in one piece, more or less."

He nodded thoughtfully. She thought he seemed about to say something else, but then Cherry called. "Emily, come on. Time to get going."

"Coming," she called back.

Alex moved swiftly around the mare till he was standing in front of her. Emily raised hesitant eyes to his. Why did they shine like that? she wondered. What was he thinking? "I'll be watching you," he told her softly.

To her surprise, he dropped a quick kiss on her forehead. "See you later," he said, then stepped back so she could move out.

His kiss burned on her forehead as she led Gypsy toward the chutes and the waiting calves. No man, except her father in the beginning, had ever come to watch her compete, had been there to give her support. The others she had known had been like Jerry, condescending, treating her like a child, discounting the importance of anything she was doing. Sudden tears blurred her eyes. It was good, very good, to have someone behind her, to have his support.

She wiped away the tears with the back of her hand.

Today she was going to outdo herself. She was going to make the best time ever.

Once in the box, she checked her horn knot once more, set the piggin' string between her teeth and adjusted her loop. Then she jammed her Stetson down hard on her head, backed Gypsy into the corner and gave the nod that indicated she was ready.

The next seconds flew by so fast that everything was a blur. Yet afterward she would remember pieces of the action like slow-motion reruns. The calf lit out and Gypsy went after him. Her loop went out at just the right angle and settled easily around the calf's neck. She was throwing out the slack and jumping off the mare's back before Gypsy could slide to a complete stop, then she went running down the rope toward the calf.

Everything around her had faded. She had no thoughts of the arena, the judges, the onlookers. Not even any thoughts of Alex. Her mind was one intense point of concentration. Get to the calf, get the right leverage, flip and tie. Her hands worked automatically, one under the belly, the other near the far front leg. The calf came down. A loop over one front foot, gather two more, a couple wraps and a half hitch. Then, hands in the air, up on her feet and the satisfied walk back to the proud mare and the sure knowledge that she had done well. "Time for Emily Asperson twelve point one seconds," said the announcer. "That little girl sure knows her stuff."

It was only the time that mattered to her, she thought as she mounted the mare again. She had not been a little girl for some time, but there was no sense in saying anything to the announcer about it. He used a certain spiel that the audience responded to, and the fact that it sometimes made fun of the women contestants in ways an announcer would never have used with men was just something they had to live with. If their plan worked, maybe things would be different. At least they were going to do something.

The rest of the afternoon passed quickly. With Cherry, the best heeler she'd ever had, she team-roped three calves in very good time, the best for the day. And during her second and third go-rounds in calf roping, Emily did very well. So well, in fact, that when the calf roping was over, the announcer proclaimed her the winner in that event.

She rubbed Gypsy's neck as she led her behind the chutes and began to unsaddle her. "You're just a wonderful horse," she crooned, stroking the mare's soft nose. "The most wonderful horse in the world." The mare's liquid brown eyes gazed into hers lovingly and Emily laid her cheek against the velvet softness. "I love you, too, Gypsy," she whispered.

Love. She was quite sure the mare loved her. And she knew she returned that love. Until now that had been all she needed. All she wanted. But now it was different. Now something had changed her. Someone had changed her, she thought, her eyes closed. And that someone was Alex Calloway. She hadn't even known the man for two whole days, but already she was aware of the difference. She wanted to be with him.

A slow flush spread to her cheeks as she realized how much she had gloried in the sight of Alex's grinning face after her victories. If she hadn't been mounted, she might easily have run right into his arms in her joy. She could not do that now, of course. Well, she *could*, but she knew she wouldn't. With a sinking heart she realized that if Alex asked her to forego a competition to go dancing with him, it would be a very different story than it had been with Jerry. She would be sorely tempted.

Her mind puzzled over this as she unsaddled the mare and rubbed her down. Alex Calloway had never even kissed her. He had caught her in his arms the other day because she'd stumbled. If just resting in his arms could do that to her, what would happen if he did kiss her? Of course, he might not. He might only be a friendly person, just enjoying her company. But there had been something in his eyes when he looked at her, something more than friendliness surely.

She sighed deeply. This whole line of thought was stupid. She should be thinking about the rodeo, about their plan, about anything except a man who was only going to be around for a little while, a man she would never see again after he finished his assignment. That thought made her almost physically ill and she pushed it aside.

"Hi, there, champ." His voice, so deep-timbered and melodious, trembled down her spine.

She turned. "Hi." He was close behind her, too close.

"It was a good day, huh?"

She nodded. "Very good." There was no need to tell him that the good didn't all come from having won.

"Worth giving your biggest fan a hug?" His eyes danced with laughter—and something else.

She managed a little laugh herself, though she was so nervous she was sure it sounded artificial. "I guess so." Why, she wondered, when she wanted more than anything in this world to be in his arms again, was she hesitating?

"Only guess?" His voice changed, became gruff and broken. "There, I shouted myself hoarse, and look at the reward I get! I shouted so much that more than one spectator looked at me askance." He pulled his features into an exaggerated expression of dismay that made her giggle nervously.

"Askance?" she asked with a raised eyebrow.

He shrugged. "You know how writers are. We like to throw words around."

"Yes."

"But we can also stick to the point. I was a vocal and vociferous supporter." She knew he used those words on purpose, too. "And now I want my reward. That doesn't seem unreasonable, does it?"

"Not at all," she conceded, and before she could lose her nerve she stepped into the arms he opened for her.

They closed around her in what was, for the moment at least, a real bear hug. Her own arms went around his lean waist.

Her head buried against his shoulder, she inhaled the fresh, clean scent of him, soap and sunshine, with a hint of leather. Her breasts were crushed against his slightly damp shirt and she could feel his strong thighs pressing against hers.

For a long minute they stood so. Torn by conflicting emotions, she tried to analyze the chaos of feeling that held her in its grip. She felt helpless and at the same time safe. Terribly excited, yet somehow at peace. It made no sense at all. But one thing was clear to her. Whether he was a stranger or not, whether he was leaving tomorrow or next week, she wanted him more than she had known it was possible to want a man.

She knew she should move, should indicate to him that she wanted to be released, but her longing held her immobile. Held her until she heard his whisper against her ear. "There now, that wasn't so bad. From what I understand, male competitors get a lot more from their fans."

She had to move then. And she forced herself to meet his eyes, even though she could feel her cheeks blazing. "You're right about that," she said lightly, as lightly as she could. "But we women don't seem to go in for that sort of thing."

"I'm glad," he whispered and the light that burned in his eyes impelled her to raise her lips to his.

They had not quite met when Cherry's cheerful call announced her arrival. "Hey, Em? You in there?"

Reluctantly she answered, "Yes, Cherry."

Just as reluctantly, it seemed, his hands fell away from her back. His expression grew rueful, but all he said was, "Time to celebrate."

She nodded. "Cherry and I usually eat together afterward even if we're not riding home together."

He nodded. "Let's go." With a last pat to Gypsy they left the box stall.

Cherry stood outside, her freckled face beaming. "We're pretty good," she announced. "If I do say so myself."

Alex chuckled as he grabbed each of them by the hand. "Come on, you terrific ropers, you, this old tenderfoot is going to treat you to the best dinner in town."

Cherry turned to her friend. "Gee, Em, where'd you get this guy? He's a real gem. The kind I run into always expect *me* to pay."

Emily joined in the general laughter, but all the way to the steak house, she was conscious of his fingers holding hers, of the good feelings that generated in her. And the bad feelings caused by the knowledge that his other hand held Cherry's and by the unusual brightness in her friend's eyes.

She was being foolish and she knew it. Cherry was just enjoying the good male companionship. Like she was. Only, Emily could not help hoping, not *quite* like she was. Not with this catch near her heart and these feelings of desolation when he looked at someone else.

Those feelings left her, fortunately, when they parted after the meal. Cherry went to load up and Emily returned to the stall for Gypsy. With Alex to help her she was able to load up her tack in a hurry. As usual, Gypsy went placidly up the ramp into the trailer. Emily fastened the door and turned to him. "All set."

He nodded. "Me, too. Say, do you want me to drive for a while?"

"Have you pulled a trailer much?"

"No."

"Then I'd better drive."

"Sorry."

He looked so crestfallen that she almost wished she'd taken him up on his offer, but that would have been foolish. "That's okay," she replied, giving him a warm smile. "You can talk and help me stay awake. That is, if I get sleepy. Right now I'm feeling pretty good."

"That's a deal," he said, his expression lightening.

He had to be useful, she thought as she pulled away from the arena. Alex was not the kind of man to go along for a free ride. He had to pull his weight.

And pull it he did. When they came to a stop in the ranch yard sometime after midnight, she was wide-awake. In short order Gypsy was turned into the corral. "I'll get the tack in the morning," she said as she shut the corral gate.

"Okay."

The ranch yard was a little dark in spite of a

generous moon and he took her elbow as they crossed to the wide porch. Her heart was already pounding in her throat and she felt so weak in the knees that she was glad of the support of his arm.

At the front door she turned to face him. "Thank you."

"Thank you," he returned. "I had a great day. It was kind of you to take me along."

She laughed softly. "Kind? After all you did?" Without thinking she reached out to touch his cheek. Only when her fingers registered the warm bristles of his beard did she realize what she was doing and draw her hand back as though it had been burned.

His eyes grew darker. "I like being your fan," he said softly.

She nodded. She searched her mind, but she could find no words that would not give away the intensity of her feelings.

"Good night," he said. The words were a mere whisper. "We'll begin lessons in the morning?"

She nodded, trying to concentrate on his words, not on the mouth so tantalizingly close to hers. "Yes. But you'll probably want to sleep late."

"What time do you usually begin?" he asked.

"E-eight." The sound of his voice was doing incredible things to her body.

"Then I'll see you at eight."

For a moment longer he stood there, looking at her. Then, abruptly, suddenly, he spun on his heel and hurried off toward the bunkhouse.

For a long moment she stood, half-paralyzed, then she turned slowly and made her way inside. To her surprise, she was not disappointed. She had expected him to kiss her, hoped he would. And in that last moment it had seemed he would.

But she could not feel bad that he hadn't. For in that last moment, his eyes had been open to hers. And in them she had read desire, a desire as strong as her own. Whatever his reason for not kissing her this evening, he would kiss her—eventually. That much was inevitable, she thought, as she stripped off her clothes and fell into bed. Yes, she told herself as she drifted off to sleep. They would kiss—and soon.

5

❦❦❦❦❦❦❦❦❦

Emily awoke early the next morning. As she opened her eyes, she found that she was smiling. Today they would begin Alex's lessons.

The days sped by. On Tuesday Alex learned how to handle the rope; on Wednesday he practiced on foot, throwing his loop, first over a bucket and then at a plastic calf head attached to a bale of hay; on Thursday morning he moved to horseback. They practiced for several hours. Alex was quick to pick things up, Emily thought, watching him through critical eyes as his loop dropped neatly over the plastic head.

She swung up on Gypsy and crossed the yard to where Alex was coiling his rope. He looked up and greeted her with a smile. "How'm I doing?"

Her own smile bubbled to the surface. She no longer fought the good feelings she had when she was with him. Fighting them had done her no good, so she had finally decided just to enjoy his company while she could.

"You're doing very well," she said. His hands were no longer so white. The hours in the sun had begun to tan them, had begun to darken his face, too, though not to the habitual bronze of a real range man.

"In fact," she went on, "you're doing so well that it's time we moved out onto the prairie. Where there's a real herd."

He nodded. "When do we go?"

She looked at her watch. "It's ten now. After lunch, I guess."

"Can't we take lunch along?" His eyes didn't meet hers quite directly. "Just peanut butter and jelly," he said, his grin widening. "Then we could practice longer."

She paused, considering. "Sounds like a good idea. Dad's away for the day. That means Mom won't have to cook lunch." She turned Gypsy toward the house. "Tell you what. I'll go make the sandwiches and meet you here, in, say, half an hour." She threw a look at the brilliant blue sky. "Better fill a canteen and bring a slicker, just in case. You'll find both in the cupboard in the bunkhouse."

"It's a deal," he said. "And don't get too elaborate with that lunch. I meant what I said about peanut butter and jelly."

She laughed. "That's good. Because that's exactly what I intend to make. Oh, will you fill my canteen, too? It's hanging in the tack room. Has my initial on it."

"Right," he said. "See you in half an hour."

Minutes later she was in the kitchen, spreading peanut butter and jelly lavishly on thick slices of her mother's homemade bread and humming softly. She supposed she ought to be feeling sad. The week was half-over already and she didn't know when Alex meant to leave. But somehow, when she was with him, she could only think of the moment.

She cut and wrapped big pieces of the chocolate cake her mother had baked the day before, added a couple oranges and apples to the bag and hurried upstairs to wash her face and tell her mother about their plans.

She made it back to the corral several minutes early and had stowed their lunch and was fastening her own slicker behind the saddle when Alex came up with the two full canteens. "Thank you," she said, suddenly afraid to meet his eyes. She secured her canteen and swung up. "Ready?"

"Ready," he replied and followed her out of the ranch yard toward the prairie.

"I think I saw a bunch of calves over that way." She indicated the direction with her hand. Alex rode beside her, so close that his knee occasionally brushed hers. Butcher Boy had taken to his new rider; he appeared to be a very different horse. There were no high jinks now. The bay was all obedience.

They took their time, moving at a walk across the prairie's verdant carpet of grass.

"It's beautiful," Alex said once. "Endless waves of grass. Or so it seems."

"It seemed that way to the first settlers, I guess. Some old Indian stories say the grass used to be taller than a horse's back." She gazed out over the prairie. "It doesn't get that tall now. Wild as this land looks, a lot of it was once plowed."

She sighed. "When the railroad came west, it brought a lot of get-rich-quick schemers with it. I

suppose some of them were honest, but any cattle-
man knew the land wouldn't support farming. A lot of
them tried to say so. And not just to save the range,
either."

She was silent, thinking of the desecration of virgin
prairie and the horrible price men had paid for it.

"What happened?"

"Oh, the railroads advertised in the newspapers.
Easterners came out to settle and farm the land—
homesteaders. They were nicknamed 'honyockers'—
hayseeds, rubes. Stupid and undesirable, is what the
word means. They weren't, really," she continued.
"They just got taken in by all the extravagant advertis-
ing and so-called dry farming methods. Also, there
was plenty of rain for a few years and wheat did
flourish."

"When did all this happen?" he asked.

"They started really pushing around 1908," she
replied. "And it went on clear into 1918. They needed
wheat during World War One, of course." She sighed
again. "After that, the drought years started and more
and more farmers had to give up and leave. You can't
grow wheat without enough rain. Wheat's not like the
buffalo grass, whose roots go deep, deep into the soil.
Buffalo grass can go a long time without rain."

The look he gave her was thoughtful. "You love this
country, don't you."

"Of course." The question took her by surprise.
"How could anyone not love it?"

"How did you learn so much about it?"

"We take Montana history in school." Her eyes met
his. "We're pretty new, as states go. And we're very
proud of our past."

He seemed about to say something more, but just
then they rounded a small slope and came upon a

little herd of cattle. Emily loosened her rope. "Now watch."

She put the mare to a canter. The cattle did not move. They were used to the presence of cowboys. Her loop sailed out and dropped over the head of a calf that browsed at the edge of the herd. Gypsy's hooves dug into the turf of the prairie as she kept the calf from running. Emily dismounted, loosened the loop, coiled the rope and remounted. "You try it," she said. "Use a different calf."

Alex looked doubtful, but he didn't say anything. Soon another unsuspecting calf found itself with a loop around its neck. Dismounting, he released the calf and looked up at her with a smile. "Well, it's not too hard when the calf stands still."

The cattle were beginning to mill around. As they talked a bigger calf lit out, away from the herd. Emily waited only long enough to cry, "Watch!" Then she gave Gypsy a signal and they were off. She kept her eye on the calf's right ear. It was as automatic as breathing now. She swung the loop, threw it. It settled over the calf's head. She jerked the rope, then pitched the slack away. Gypsy went skidding to a stop as Emily's right boot hit the grass and she was down the rope, grasping the calf. She didn't throw it this time; Alex wasn't ready for that yet. Loosening her rope, she coiled it and mounted again.

Alex moved up to her side. "Are you sure that doesn't hurt the calf?"

She was going to make a joke of his concern, but, meeting his eyes, she saw that it was very real. "I don't think so," she replied seriously. "Ranchers have been using this method for many years. I don't think they'd do anything that would deplete their herds. They *are* businessmen, you know."

"I know."

He was still not convinced: she could see that by his face and by the way he looked at the calves as he turned toward her.

She watched him practice for an hour or so before she called a halt. "Lunchtime."

"Where do we eat?" he asked. "I've been thinking about those sandwiches all morning. I love peanut butter and jelly."

Her laughter pealed out. She was laughing a lot lately, she thought. "Let's ride on a little," she said. "Away from the cattle."

"Sure."

They rode knee to knee for about five minutes. Emily breathed deeply. "I love the smell of the prairie. It's so fresh. The wild flowers are just beautiful this time of year."

"I bet you know all their names."

She shook her head. "No, only some. Like that purple spiky stuff over there—that's lupine."

She turned to him, only to discover that his eyes were on her, not on the prairie around them. Her face turned warm as the color rose to her cheeks. "Hare-bells are pretty," she hurried on, hardly knowing what she was saying. "They're dainty little things. And over near Glacier Park arnica grows, and Indian paint-brush, and Glacier lilies." She stopped, unable to think of any more flowers to name. "Look, there's a nice spot over there."

The cattle were behind them now and they pulled the horses to a halt. Emily swung down and busied herself getting the lunch out of her saddlebags. When she turned with it and her canteen, she was surprised to see Alex unrolling a blanket.

"All the comforts of home," he said, waving her to a

67

seat. "I was a boy scout," he continued. "We always go prepared."

She dropped to the blanket and began to take out the lunch. He joined her, settling himself across from her.

He eyed the food hungrily. "Seems like years since I've eaten."

She passed him a sandwich. "It's that clear prairie air," she replied. "It braces the appetite."

"Well, it sure works. I could eat a horse."

A sudden snort from Butcher Boy startled them both. "Sorry, old fellow," Alex called. "Present company excluded, of course."

"Of course," Emily agreed. And they fell to laughing so hard that she had to put the sandwiches down and hold her ribs.

When she was finally able to stop laughing, she wiped hastily at her streaming eyes. He, too, had tears of laughter on his cheeks.

Alex swiped at them with the back of his hand before he reached for the sandwich she was offering him. "Why do you suppose we have so much fun together?" he asked.

She shook her head, dropping her eyes to the sandwich she was unwrapping for herself. "I don't know. Maybe we're both crazy."

He chuckled. "Maybe. Maybe a little bit of crazy is a help in getting along in this world. What do you think?"

She had taken a bite of sandwich now and could hardly avoid his gaze without him being conscious of it. "Maybe," she replied, raising her eyes to meet his. It was okay, she told herself. He was just looking at her normally. He hadn't meant anything special by his question. So she'd been right to suppress the first reply that had popped into her mind at his question. He would never know that she had thought of answering, "Could it be because we're falling in love?"

No, better not to say anything like that. If it were really happening, if they were falling in love—both of them and not just her—she would know soon enough. And, if the falling were all on her part, then she certainly didn't want him to know about it.

"Penny for your thoughts," he said, munching gravely.

She laughed and hoped it sounded natural. "Just trying to remember when I last ate peanut butter and jelly sandwiches."

"Can you?"

"No. It's been a long time."

"Me, too." He took another sandwich and began to unwrap it. "Can you tell me some more about the training a horse gets?" he asked. "Horses fascinate me. I know you have signals you give Gypsy, but sometimes I could swear she does it all herself."

Emily chuckled. "She really does do a lot of it." She felt more relaxed now. Talking about horses was always fun for her. "I think I told you that Dad trained her for me."

Alex nodded. "I suppose the training is quite rigorous."

The word startled her. "What do you mean?"

He seemed almost embarrassed. "Well, the horse has a lot to learn." He paused.

"Good roping horses are trained slowly," she said. "A little at a time. A good trainer knows not to rush things. Cutting and roping horses are best trained on working ranches. You can understand that."

He nodded, munching thoughtfully.

"Of course the horse has to be trained for riding first. That takes time, too."

"I always thought breaking horses was kind of painful stuff." He hesitated. "I mean, they're so beautiful, running wild and free. And the word 'breaking' seems to imply breaking their spirit."

She shook her head. "That's not necessarily so. Anyway, the old-time cowboys worked in different circumstances. A lot of the horses in the remudas were range mustangs, and ran wild. A cowboy just roped one, slapped a saddle on it and rode till it gave up. Things aren't like that now. Horses are raised to be trained specifically for certain things. Many times they're bred and raised, gentled and trained, all on the same ranch. By the time they're ready for the saddle, they don't have any fear of men."

He finished the last sandwich and crumpled the wrapper. She was glad she had made plenty. He might not be as big as her brothers, but he had a good-sized appetite. Smiling, she handed him a piece of cake.

"Then where do the bucking horses come from?" he asked.

She unwrapped a piece of cake for herself. "Different places. Some are still wild horses that have been rounded up. But not many. These days most bucking horses are bred by stockmen."

He chewed slowly. "And you say they really aren't killers?"

"That's right." He had a cake crumb on his chin. She wanted to lean over and brush it away, but she didn't dare.

His eyes were on her, those dark eyes that had held such promises. They held promises now. She swallowed hastily, trying to pull her own eyes away. "Next time you're at the rodeo, watch. You'll see. It's an exceptional bucking horse that tries to stomp a man when he's been thrown." She kept talking, afraid to keep looking at him, but unable to look away. She wanted what his eyes promised, but she was afraid. "In fact, some bucking horses quit bucking as soon as they hear the buzzer." She managed a smile. "Cowboys call them 'union' horses. Because they quit as soon as the whistle blows."

He chuckled. "The West is every bit as fascinating as I used to think." He laughed softly. "In a different way, of course. Not the cowboys and Indians, rustlers and gunfighters of my earlier days. I'm a western movie fan, of course."

"Of course." She finished her cake. "What's your absolute most favorite western movie?" she asked, knowing as she did so that she didn't really want to talk about movies, that she didn't really want to talk at all. She wanted to be in his arms, to be held close, to feel . . .

He frowned, his forehead creasing. "I don't have to think long about that," he replied. "It's *Shane.* There was never a braver, stronger, cleaner, righter cowboy than Alan Ladd in *Shane.*"

She couldn't help herself; delighted laughter bubbled out of her. "He's my favorite actor, even though he died when I was very young."

He nodded. "TV has kept the old great ones alive." He seemed about to add something, then decided against it.

It came to her suddenly in a flash of insight and her gasp of surprise was clearly audible.

"What is it?" he asked.

"Your voice! Your voice is like his!" She was too

stunned to dissemble. "The minute I heard it, I knew I'd heard it before. It was hauntingly familiar, but I didn't know why."

He laughed, then, and she thought his fingers trembled slightly as he brushed at imaginary crumbs. "That's how I discovered his movies. Someone told me that I sounded like him. So I watched the next one to come on TV and I was hooked."

She shivered there in the sunlight. It seemed incredible that she should find someone who shared her feelings for an actor long dead. "My brothers always laugh at western movies," she said. "They pick them all to pieces." She swallowed hastily. "They don't see the spirit of the thing. There's a West that exists only in the American imagination. It's glorified and enriched, maybe. But it symbolizes our past, our history."

He nodded. "That's right. And who knows about history, anyway? It's always a representation, not the reality." He paused. "Did you study film-making?"

She nodded. "A little. I liked it, but I couldn't face the idea of Hollywood and the Los Angeles Freeway. Too many people. Too many cars. Too much of everything."

She looked down at the rest of their lunch. "Would you like some more cake? Or a piece of fruit?"

He shook his head. "Nope. I'm stuffed." He grinned. "That was my favorite childhood lunch. Peanut butter and jelly sandwiches and chocolate cake. I don't want to spoil it by eating a 'should' food like fruit." His eyes glittered with mischief. "I would like to sit here a while longer, though, and see what other interests we have in common."

Her heart pounded in her throat, but she managed to keep her hands steady while she packed away the remaining food and gathered up the discarded wrappings. She set the bag to one side and swallowed. Anxiety was flooding over her again. She wanted him to kiss her; there was no point in denying it.

"When you were little did you ever lie on your back and watch the clouds?" he asked.

"Sometimes I did." Her lips felt stiff, as though they didn't want to frame the words. She knew she was being silly. She'd been out with men before. But none who affected her like this one, some part of her mind reminded her.

"Let's do it now," he suggested. "Let's lie down." His hand closed over hers, pulling her down on the blanket beside him.

When they were lying side by side, his fingers still around hers, he said, "Now what do you see?"

There was only one wispy white cloud in the entire brilliant blue sky, but she tried to concentrate on it. "I . . . It's been too long," she said finally. "I can only see a little cloud."

He rolled suddenly toward her and, propping himself on his elbow, gazed down at her. "I'd rather look at you, anyway," he said. "Do you know how beautiful you are?"

She felt the blood flooding to her cheeks and was powerless to stop it. Just as she was powerless to pull her eyes away from his. It *was* almost like drowning, she thought hazily as she fought to keep control of herself. "Alan Ladd wouldn't have said that." She barely managed to get the words out and they lacked the lightness she had hoped for.

"No. He wouldn't have *said* anything." His lips were very close to hers. His eyes darkened. "But he would have *done* this."

As his lips touched hers, her arms went automatically around his neck. It seemed right, that kiss, and more exciting than any kiss she had ever experienced. Her heart pounded so hard that she was sure he could feel it against his chest, the chest that was now pressed against her breasts.

His mouth was gentle and persuasive, tender yet urgent. Her body clamored for the feel of his, for more and more of this joy.

When he released her, she lay shaken until he gathered her against his side. "I suppose I should apologize," he said. "Presuming on our brief acquaintance like that."

She didn't say anything. With his arm around her and his body holding her close, she wasn't sure she could speak coherently.

He chuckled softly and kissed the top of her head. "But the truth is, I've been wanting to do that since the first time I laid eyes on you."

6

By the time they rode back into the ranch yard it was midafternoon and Emily had regained some semblance of calm. Glancing at Alex riding so easily beside her, the whole thing almost seemed like a dream. Could she really have been lying there beside him on the prairie, kissing and being kissed, talking about scenes in Alan Ladd movies, feeling Alex's arms around her, his cheek against hers?

He turned in the saddle and flashed her a warm smile and she found herself smiling back. She had never felt this kind of rapport with a man, she thought, as she considered the intensity of her feelings for this stranger.

"Company?" Alex asked, gesturing toward the back corral where two tall, rangy cowboys were deep in conversation.

Emily looked that way. "No. The boys . . . my brothers are home. Come on, I'll introduce you."

Ted turned as they came up. "Hello, squirt. Where've you been?"

"Out riding," she replied, swinging down. She disliked the nickname "squirt." She was twenty-five years old, not a little kid. As Ted well knew.

Joe grinned. "Hi, Sis. How come you weren't here to welcome the conquering heroes?"

She managed a laugh. Ordinarily her brothers' bravado didn't bother her, but now she was acutely conscious of Alex, of what he would think of them. "I guess that means you've been winning," she said.

"What else? Gonna be champion this year."

Ted guffawed. "Ah, go on. Your chaps are carrying dirt from half the arenas in this part of the country."

"And what about yours?"

Emily sent Alex a tired smile. "They're always like this. Just two overgrown kids."

Her brothers turned on her.

"Watch what you're saying there, kiddo." Joe scowled threateningly.

But Ted burst into laughter. "Better take it easy, Joe. I remember what happened the last time you tangled with her."

Joe tried to hold the scowl but couldn't and ended up grinning. "Okay, I admit it. She's one tough customer."

They both looked at her expectantly. "Alex, these are my brothers. Joe and Ted. And this is Alex Calloway. He's learning to rope."

"From you?"

"From me," she replied, more sharply than she'd intended to. But it was hard being put down all the time. She was a better roper than either of her brothers. Even her father said so. But they persisted in treating her like a child.

"Emily is a very good teacher." Alex's voice seemed deeper than usual and her brothers almost stared. It was an unusual voice for any man and Alex was not particularly tall or broad. "I'm pleased to meet you," he continued. "If you have time, I'd like to discuss the rodeo with you."

"Alex is writing a book," Emily explained.

"About the rodeo?" asked Joe.

"Yes."

"What kind of a book?"

Alex frowned. "I'm not exactly sure yet. Nonfiction, though."

Emily felt a vague sense of uneasiness. Why was it that when Alex spoke about his book he seemed to change, to withdraw into himself? And why didn't he ever get more specific about it? Surely by now he knew how the book would go.

But maybe he didn't like to discuss his work beforehand. Maybe that spoiled it for him. She had known some photographers who were that way, very closemouthed about their projects until they were finished. Some had even been superstitious, feeling that talking about it beforehand would spoil a layout.

She turned her attention back to the men. With Alex between them, her brothers were approaching the corral. Now she saw the horses in it. New horses. They looked wild.

"Bought a few head, mostly wild," Joe was saying. "Figured to break 'em ourselves."

"I see." Alex's tone was noncommittal.

"You ride much?" asked Ted, with a sidelong glance at his brother.

"A little," Alex admitted. "I've never done any breaking, though."

"Nothing to it," Joe said. "We'll tell you what to do."

"Well . . ."

Emily's heart rose up in her mouth. Surely Alex couldn't be that gullible. Of course he could ride, but that didn't mean he'd be any good at breaking rough stock. He was apt to get thrown, hurt even. "I don't think—"

"Say, squirt," Ted interrupted. "How about getting us some cold ones?"

"I don't—"

"Come on, Sis." It was Joe's turn to interrupt. "You're not being very hospitable."

She was about to protest again when Alex turned to her. "Make mine soda pop," he said, and, as her brothers exchanged a knowing look over the top of his head, he winked broadly.

She gave up attempting to protest then. That wink made it clear to her that Alex knew what was going on.

"Right," she said, sending her brothers a baleful look. They really were acting like overgrown kids, trying to put the new boy down.

Of course, as soon as Alex spoke they could tell he wasn't a westerner. And his face, though it was tanned, didn't have the bronzed look of a man who habitually rode the range.

Grimly she opened the refrigerator, took two cans of beer out of it, then two cans of pop. She shook her head. Soda pop! Had Alex really known what he was doing? Had he asked for soda pop deliberately? If her brothers hadn't already marked him for a tenderfoot, that had certainly done the job.

And then it hit her. Soda pop! Shane had asked for soda pop in the cattlemen's saloon. She recalled the scene now. He'd been dressed in his new homesteading clothes and not wearing his guns. They'd laughed at him, those cattlemen who hated the homesteaders he was trying to help. But he hadn't been the weakling they thought. And neither was Alex. That was what he was trying to tell her.

Some of the grimness faded from her features. Maybe all the setting up wasn't on her brothers' side. Maybe Alex had a trick or two up his sleeve. She hoped so. She picked up the cans and turned back toward the door.

The men were still standing outside the corral. From the looks on their faces, Joe and Ted were having a lot of fun. Alex's expression was polite; she could read nothing more from it.

Ted and Joe took their beers and snapped them open. As Alex reached for his can of pop his eyes met hers once more. He was trying to tell her something. It was going to be interesting to see who was the most surprised. She had a feeling that her brothers were in for a shock.

"I'll saddle her up," said Joe, handing Ted his half-empty can.

Watching over the rim of her can, Emily kept silent. Her brothers wouldn't listen to her and Alex was determined to play this charade through to the end. And it was going to be a very different end from what her brothers envisioned, she suspected.

The mare stood quietly enough as Joe slipped the hackamore over her head. She didn't even move much when he put the saddle on her back. In fact, thought Emily, this mare was behaving very strangely for a wild one. She eyed it critically—a nondescript dun, no special markings. But there was something familiar about her.

It came to her as Joe was ushering Alex through the

gate. That was not just a wild horse in there; that was Loop-the-Loop, a celebrated bucking horse. Anxiety washed over her again. Did Alex really know what he was getting into?

He struggled into the saddle with an awkwardness so exaggerated that she had to cough to cover her rising laughter. The mare seemed almost surprised by his clumsiness, just standing there for several seconds. Joe used her hesitation to beat a judicious retreat, getting himself outside the fence in double-quick time.

Suddenly the mare exploded, all four legs leaving the ground as she sunfished. Unbelievably, the figure on her back remained there. The shock, as all her feet returned to the ground, rippled through him visibly. But there was hardly time to absorb it before the mare launched into another series of jolting, bone-jarring maneuvers, designed to unseat the most skilled rider.

And still Alex stayed on the horse. He didn't attempt the spurring action of the rodeo cowboy or the one-handed stance, but he stayed on. He stayed on for some seconds past the usual eight, until the dun mare, perhaps wondering why the buzzer didn't sound, suddenly stopped and just stood there.

There was no awkwardness to the figure that swung down and moved to her head with one practiced motion. "She's good," Alex said. "Are you planning to breed her?"

For a moment both Emily's brothers seemed struck speechless. Then they looked at each other and burst into laughter. "Well, you ain't such a tenderfoot after all," Joe said as he went to uncinch the saddle. "You really put one over on us."

Alex's grin was just as boyish and mischievous as theirs. "I don't like getting all dirty," he said. "And you didn't even offer day money."

For some reason this sent them all off into fresh spasms of laughter. Emily could only watch in amazement. Men sometimes behaved in peculiar ways. Like when two of them had a knock-down-drag-out match, beating each other bloody, and then afterward walked away, the best of friends. There was no understanding such creatures, she thought, as her brothers, now convinced of Alex's right to full acceptance, began to discuss with him the horses they had bought.

Later that evening, after a dinner during which Joe and Ted had treated Alex like a long-lost brother, Emily stood in the dimness of the stable, her fingers absently stroking Gypsy's nose. She had come out to check on her horse; since she was rodeoing the next day that made sense. But actually she had come out into the stable's peaceful silence to think.

She had always found it easier to think in the company of horses. Their quiet companionship had always been comforting to her. There was something about their complete acceptance of her that made thinking easier. It had been that way for as long as she could remember. Even in the winter, she often deserted the warm house to sit in the stable with its smell of leather and horses. Many a tough problem had been worked out, there in the stable.

Her fingers continued their absent stroking of Gypsy's nose as her thoughts returned to the day's events. Their picnic lunch had been almost enchanted, a scene out of an old movie. She would treasure the memory forever.

But it seemed already shrouded in the hazy vagueness of the distant past. Alex did not seem the same man since she had seen him with her brothers.

She sighed. Why did her feelings have to be so

ambivalent? Of course she wanted her brothers to like Alex. He was her friend. And if he ever became anything more . . . She pushed that thought aside. She should have been very pleased to see him getting along with them so well. She had felt a sense of triumph that he had ridden the bucking mare to a standstill, but that had quickly faded as her brothers had taken over, monopolizing the conversation with him and treating her comments like the interruptions of a rude child. She knew just as much about horses as they did, but they would never admit it. She frowned there in the stillness and sighed again.

"What's wrong with men, anyway?" she asked the mare. "Why can't they meet a woman as an equal and not always be trying to put her in her so-called place?"

The mare whuffled softly and reached across the bars to nuzzle her neck.

"I am so tired of being treated like a child," Emily went on to the sympathetic mare. "It's disgusting. I don't see why they can't recognize that I'm grown up."

They would see, though, a part of her mind reminded her. When the plan was successful, those stubborn men would see. She laid her cheek against the mare's soft nose. "Guess we'd better both get some rest. After all, we're competing tomorrow."

She turned and gasped. A figure lounged in the doorway. "I didn't mean to startle you," Alex said. His face was in the shadow but she could see the whiteness of his teeth as he grinned. "And I didn't mean to interrupt a private conversation."

Any other time she would have laughed with him, but now, still smarting at having been excluded from the dinner conversation, she snapped back, "At least Gypsy listens to what I have to say."

He came toward her, his face emerging from the shadows. "I'm sorry about that," he said, his expression serious. "But I thought you'd want your brothers to like me."

Her heart rose up in her throat. Why should she want that unless . . .

"I'd really much rather have talked to you," he went on.

Her irritation vanished. Here was the Alex of their prairie picnic. "I didn't mean to grouch at you," she apologized. "It's not your fault. Most of the men around here are like that."

Alex shook his head. "It doesn't make sense to me. But listen, I came out to talk about tomorrow. I hear there's a rodeo at Brockway. Want to ride over with me and take a look?"

"I'd like to, Alex, but I'm competing myself. Down at Miles City. I meant to tell you at dinner. I was going to leave you to practice on your own." She didn't add the words echoing in her mind: though I hoped you'd come with me.

He was close to her now. She could see his frown clearly. "Shoot! I wanted to spend the day together."

She was tempted to give up the plan, to spend the day with him. But this wasn't just for her. There were ten women with their money and their hope invested in this thing. And to even have a chance at succeeding, she had to compete every time she could.

So she kept silent and remained still, though she was longing to take the two short steps that would bring her into his arms.

The silence lengthened and grew into a tangible thing, hanging there between them. She wanted to say something, anything, to drive it away, but no words would come.

Finally he spoke. "Well, then, if the mountain won't come to Mohammed, Mohammed will have to go to the mountain."

Her heart gave a quick bound, but she forced herself to be sensible, to think of him. "I don't want to interfere with your work. This is just a woman's rodeo."

He shook his head. "Emily Asperson, listen to you. Why, you sound as bad as those macho brothers of yours. Just a woman's rodeo, indeed."

He took another step toward her. He was so close, her hands longed to reach out and touch him, to feel the strength of that lean body.

"All right," she said. "But we'll have to leave at five."

A strange, closed look passed over his face. "I've got a couple of things I have to do in the morning. I'll meet you there."

"Okay."

He frowned thoughtfully. "I may not be there in time to talk to you beforehand. But I will be there. Will you watch for me?"

"Of course."

His voice had dropped a tone, to that intimate timbre that sent all her nerves tingling. She wanted him to kiss her, she wanted it desperately, but she was powerless to move.

Then his hands were reaching out, drawing her close against his chest. She could feel his heart beating against her breast. Her own heart was pounding. "Thank you for the picnic," he said softly, his lips against hers. "It was marvelous. Like something out of a movie."

She raised her eyes to his. "This afternoon, by the corral, when you asked for a soda pop . . ."

"Yes?" His eyes twinkled in the dimness.

"Like in *Shane?*"

He laughed softly and hugged her. "I knew you'd get it."

"I almost didn't. I was worried about you."

"You've seen me handle Butcher Boy."

"But a bucking horse is different." She found herself smiling. "You looked so innocent. Such a tenderfoot."

He chuckled. "I've been around long enough to know when I'm being set up."

"You enjoyed it!"

"Of course," he said. "Didn't you?"

"In a way. But Butcher Boy's just a little frisky. I didn't know if you could handle a real bucking horse."

His expression grew a little sheepish. "Neither did I. But I wanted to find out."

She stared at him. "You mean you've never . . ."

"I've never ridden a bucking horse. Oh, my gelding used to kick up his heels on occasion, but nothing like old Loop-the-Loop."

"You recognized her?"

"Pure luck." Alex grinned. "She worked in a rodeo I caught a couple of weeks ago."

She shook her head. "You could have been hurt."

He shrugged. "Life is like that," he said, repeating a sentiment she herself had expressed. "You have to take chances in order to really live. Besides, you can get hurt falling out of your bed. And what fun would that be?"

"Alex Calloway," she began, but she got no further, for he chose that moment to bend his head and cover her lips with his. Her arms stole around his neck and she pressed herself against him.

The afternoon seemed to reenact itself there in his

arms. His lips were warm on hers, warm and eager, and his hands moved from her waist to her hips, pulling her body even tighter against his. Desire shot through her, leaving her breathless. She wanted him with every fiber of her being. But nothing could make her forget where they stood. Or the fact that someone could come upon them at any moment.

She pulled her mouth free. "Alex." His name was sweet on her tongue. "We mustn't. My brothers . . ."

He didn't try to regain her mouth, but it was several seconds before his hands fell away from her body. "And how old did you say you are?" He was still breathing heavily.

"I'm twenty-five," she replied. "And I know it's silly. But there are two of them. And only one of you." She raised a trembling hand to his cheek and chuckled. "Even Shane backed off when he was outnumbered."

That brought the smile she was looking for. He took a step backward, away from her. "All right, I hear you. Say, your brothers aren't going to Miles City to watch you tomorrow, are they?"

She shook her head and her heart began to pound again. "Not a chance. They wouldn't waste their time."

Now she was sure she saw the twinkle in his eyes. That, and something more. Something that almost made her forget her own arguments and move back into his arms. But she forced herself to remain away from him. It might sound amusing, but if Joe and Ted teamed up to knock some sense into a man—as they would put it—even Shane would be hard put to defend himself. Anyway, this wasn't a movie, this was reality. And the last thing she wanted was to see this man hurt, this man she cared so much about.

She smiled at him. "I'd better go in."

He nodded. "If you say so."

His words were innocent enough, but the message in his eyes made her flesh tremble and her blood race. She half turned, reluctant to leave him, yet knowing she must.

Blowing her a whimsical kiss, he whispered, "Till tomorrow, then."

7

Emily glanced at her watch. Not even a minute had passed since she had looked last. But it was getting late. Where was Alex?

"Em. Em!" Cherry's voice betrayed her exasperation. "Where's your mind? You haven't heard a word I've been saying."

Emily turned to face her friend, who was sitting beside her on the top rail of a fence. Shifting her weight and automatically hooking a foot over the bottom railing, she smiled weakly. "Sorry. I'm not with it today."

Cherry's gaze grew critical. "You look like something the cat dragged in." She smiled suddenly. "That new man been keeping you out late?"

Emily shook her head. Cherry was a good friend, but she could not keep a secret. And there was no use in everyone in Jordan gossiping about her and Alex. He would be gone soon, anyway. . . .

She pushed that thought out of her mind. Cherry was right. She did look tired. And no wonder. She'd hardly slept all night, thinking of Alex, thinking of his kisses, of the promise in his eyes.

It had certainly been clear to her that she wanted him. As clear as the fact that he wanted her. What was not clear, what had kept her tossing and turning till the sheets were a tangled mess, was what she should do about it.

She had never been one to sleep around and it was plain enough that Alex would soon be moving on. His very profession indicated that. Always before she had refused men like that, men without permanence and stability. That was the thing she most disliked about Jerry and his kind. Rodeo cowboys were always on the move, always going on down the road to a new place, a new contest. Much as she liked competing, she could not see herself forever on the road.

With Alex it would only be slightly different. There would not be the ever-present fear of his getting hurt. But his life-style was basically the same. A lot of travel. No permanence.

Her eyes unseeing, she gazed out over the arena. She had reviewed all the facts, all the arguments pro and con. And she had come to her decision. If Alex came to Miles City, if Alex wanted her, she was going to be with him. It might not be sensible; her mind told her it wasn't. But she no longer cared. She was twenty-five years old. There were no men in her life that had half the attraction for her that he did. There never had been. And just this once she was going to please herself.

If their passion were fleeting, if he would soon be gone out of her life, she would handle it. If love could only be found in the arms of a stranger, then that's the way it would be. She was willing to accept that.

She didn't like it, the knowledge that she was close to loving this man, this stranger. But she knew it was true. And basically she could understand why. Alex was different from the men she knew. He could be tough and hard if necessity demanded it, but he also had a sensitive, tender side. She smiled suddenly as she realized that she was again comparing Alex's character to that of the mythical Shane—and finding them very similar. Not only did he have a voice like Alan Ladd's; he had a personality like the kind of man Ladd had so beautifully portrayed—a mixture of tough and tender.

She not only wanted Alex. She liked him. She respected him. So if he asked, she was going to be ready.

Her thoughts flew back to her good-byes that morning. Her mother had come down to the kitchen to wish her good luck and to ask when to expect her back. A slight pink tinged Emily's cheeks as she remembered her reply. Did her mother really believe what she'd told her? That she wasn't sure exactly when she'd be home. That she wanted to do some shopping in Miles City and might stay the night. The look on her mother's face had been strange. She'd even opened her mouth as though to say something, then had closed it again with a snap and just nodded.

"Em!" The insistent tone of Cherry's voice let her know that she'd been daydreaming again.

"Sorry, Cherry. I'm just off my feed today."

"I hope you're not off your roping," her friend replied, her voice holding a hint of acid. "I need some day money."

"I know. I'll concentrate. Really I will."

"You'd better." Cherry's smile took the sting out of her words. "It isn't just me, you know." She looked around and dropped her voice. "There's the plan to be considered. We're all counting on you.'

"I know." She hoped Cherry didn't hear the tiredness in her voice. She didn't know if she could do anything right. Her eyes scanned the crowd again. Where was he? Why couldn't she see him?

"Time to go," Cherry said.

"I'm ready." Emily tried to put Alex out of her mind. This was serious business, this competition. It meant a lot to Cherry. And to the other girls, too. She mounted, coiled her rope and tried to relax some of the tenseness in her shoulders. Cherry deserved a partner who would give the roping her best shot.

As they moved into position behind the barriers, Emily fought to keep from scanning the crowd one more time. The calf—she had to think about the calf. She felt the tensing of Gypsy's muscles as the mare waited.

The calf shot out past the barrier with Gypsy right after it. Swing. Throw. Jerk. Pitch. The familiar words echoed in her mind and her body moved automatically. The throw looked good, but just as it seemed about to settle over the calf's head, the animal twisted and the loop fell to the ground.

Her second loop caught the calf's head squarely and Cherry's loop took his heels almost immediately. But they were out of the money now. It was very unlikely that all the other contestants would miss a throw and pile up so many extra seconds.

As she pulled in her loop and followed Cherry out of the arena, Emily fought to keep the tears down. She was being stupid. She'd done the best she could. Even the best ropers missed a calf now and then. It couldn't be helped. Still, she felt as though she'd let her friend down.

"Hey," Cherry said as they swung down from their horses. "Don't look so glum. It's not the end of the world. I saw that loop go out. It should have fallen right."

Strangely, Cherry's sympathy made her feel even more like crying. Emily managed a small smile. "I'm sorry, though. I like to win."

"Don't we all?" replied Cherry, her usual good spirits back in evidence. "Listen, I'm going to get a can of pop. Be back later. Okay?"

"Okay."

As she watched her friend stride off, Emily wondered if Cherry suspected how upset she really was. She hoped not.

"Bad luck," said a voice behind her, a deep voice that made the blood flood into her cheeks as she turned.

"Alex! You did come!" She stopped suddenly, aware of how much she was giving away.

"Of course. I said I would. Tough about that last calf. I thought sure you had him."

"So did I." Her eyes devoured him. He looked so handsome in his jeans and blue shirt, a dark Stetson on his fair hair. She recognized the fear that had been lingering in the back of her mind—the fear that he would not come, that she would never see him again. She swallowed hastily. Suddenly she seemed to have run out of things to say.

"Listen, I just wanted to let you know I'm here. I'll meet you after the last go-round." His eyes searched her face. "Okay?"

"Okay." She tried to look normal, unconcerned, to keep the joy off her face.

He smiled at her, then started back toward the arena. The day was suddenly much brighter, now that she had seen him, now that she knew he was there.

She turned toward the patiently waiting mare. "Oh, Gypsy," she whispered against the glossy neck. "I've got it bad. Really bad."

The mare whuffled in sympathy, turning to nuzzle her soft nose against Emily's cheek.

"Oh, Gypsy." The tears brimmed in her eyes now and Emily wasn't sure why. "Love is so complicated." She smiled as the mare shook her head from side to side, almost as though she were disagreeing. Of course the horse didn't understand, but Emily continued to talk to her. "It must be a whole lot simpler for you," she went on. "Too bad I wasn't born a horse."

A curious sense of excitement followed her through the rest of the competition. Everything seemed to go just right. On their next go-rounds, she and Cherry did exceptionally well. It wouldn't get them day money, of course. But it did help their self-esteem. And Emily was glad to hear Cherry's vibrant laugh and her "Next time we'll whomp 'em for sure," as they parted behind the chutes.

Waiting for the calf roping to begin, she tried to relax, tried not to think of Alex. But it was practically impossible. Finally she gave in, letting her eyes search the stands for his blue shirt and fair hair. She found him, eventually, down near the front, his head uncovered to the sun, fanning himself with his Stetson.

She watched him for a while. He was too far away for her to read the expression on his face, but she could tell from the set of his body how intently he was watching the arena. Then, putting his hat back on his head, he took a small notebook from his pocket and began making notes.

She was still watching him when they announced that the calf roping was about to begin. She could feel Gypsy's eagerness; the little mare loved to compete. Sometimes, Emily was sure, her horse enjoyed rodeoing more than she herself did.

Inside the chute, Gypsy backed into the corner. Sitting there, her rope coiled, the piggin' string between her teeth, Emily felt her eyes drawn again toward the stands, but this time she rejected the pull. All her thoughts, all her concentration, must be focused on the calf.

She nodded and the calf was released. Gypsy was after it, barely missing the ten-second barrier. Swing. Throw. Jerk. Pitch. The loop fell with beautiful precision around the calf's neck. Gypsy slid to a stop almost before Emily was out of the saddle, running down the rope. One hand on its front leg, up high near the belly, the other on its flank near the back leg. Heave and throw. Grab a front leg, loop it. Gather the two back ones. A couple twists and a half hitch. Her hands in the air to show she was finished.

"Nine point seven seconds." The announcer's voice floated out over the arena. "A great time for the little lady whose daddy, Joe Asperson, teaches roping over near Jordan way."

Emily retrieved her rope and went back to Gypsy. She knew that particular announcer. He had rodeoed with her father. No doubt he thought he was doing his old friend a favor, but she couldn't help hearing the implication. She was good because of a man— because her daddy had taught her.

Riding Gypsy back behind the chutes, she found herself wondering if anything would ever really change. All the men she knew would find the announcer's words perfectly acceptable. After all, she was only a girl. If she could rope well, it must be because of a man.

Emily shook her head. Not a one of them would admit it, but she was every bit as good as a man. She could rope calves with any of them. The girls had even considered trying to get a one-on-one match going, pitting her against a male roper. But they had given the idea up. You couldn't have a one-on-one unless both parties were willing. And no rodeo cowboy was going to descend to such depths, to invite the derision of his friends and buddies, by competing against a female.

Besides, she thought bitterly, they were probably afraid of losing. And if that happened . . . A cowboy would never live down losing to a woman. No, the girls had been right to forget that approach. The new plan was better. The men couldn't stop it because they wouldn't even know about it—until it was too late.

Time alternately dragged and raced as she waited for her next go-round and covertly watched Alex. She wanted the competition to be over so that she could be with him, but she also enjoyed watching him, storing up memories of the way he moved, all the little gestures that make a person distinctive.

And then it was time to go into the chute again. To back Gypsy into the corner, take the piggin' string between her teeth and uncoil her rope. She took a deep breath and thought positive thoughts. The perfect loop, the perfect calf, the perfect time. She nodded. Might as well get it over with.

The calf leaped forward, Gypsy after it so fast Emily was afraid that they hit the barrier. But there was no time to worry about that. No time to think of it, even.

The familiar litany repeated itself in her head and her body responded. Swing. Throw. Jerk. Pitch. She had done it hundreds, thousands of times.

The loop settled just as it should have and almost before it landed she was off the mare, her body moving swiftly through the rest of the routine. The calf wanted to strain and she lost a precious second recapturing a flailing leg, but it was still a very good time—10.9 seconds. She left the arena wearing a satisfied smile.

By the time she had Gypsy unsaddled and was rubbing her down, the announcer had informed the crowd that Emily Asperson had done her daddy proud and was taking home a tidy sum for her efforts in the calf roping event.

The hand that was brushing Gypsy moved a little faster and a little harder at the man's condescending tone. Emily knew he had never been able to rope as well as she could. But she swallowed the curse she felt like uttering. You never knew when an official was around, and if one of them reprimanded her for cursing she might really blow her stack and tell the whole lot of macho idiots how much like little boys they were behaving.

All but one, she thought with a secret smile. Alex was different. She didn't care if it was because of his sisters or what. She only knew that she liked talking to a man who treated her like a human being rather than some half-grown child.

And they shared so much. Their love of the West—idealized, she knew, but as long as they were aware of it, it did them no harm. Their love of the old westerns —particularly Alan Ladd's. She knew they portrayed a different West than the one she lived in—where right triumphed and wrong, no matter how superior its strength, was ultimately vanquished.

Life was not like that. There were not always happy endings. She knew that. But the world was not all gloom and doom, either. Even the worst life had some moments of joy.

"Hello." Alex's deep voice was like a caress. It seemed almost like a touch on her body.

She swung around to meet him, the brush hanging from her hand. "Hello," she replied. Not very original, but adequate, she supposed. Her eyes moved over him swiftly, taking in the dampness of his shirt, his wet forehead. He still wasn't used to so much sun.

His eyes were busy, too; they held admiration, and something more that made her breath quicken. "You were great, Emily," he said. "Really great."

"Thanks." She felt suddenly embarrassed, unable to think of anything more to say. His eyes were still on her and she swung back toward the mare, moving the brush over her glossy flank.

Though she couldn't see him, she heard him come closer, felt him just behind her. "Aren't horses great animals?" he asked. "So much beauty. So much grace." He chuckled. "I think if I believed in reincarnation, I'd want to come back as a horse."

"A swift palomino stallion," she murmured, not daring to look around at him.

"Hmmmm," he said. "I like that idea. I like it a lot."

She thought she felt a finger touch her curls.

"A palomino stallion with a passion for a little dark mare."

Her heart was pounding in her throat, but she tried for a lighthearted tone. "Sometimes a mare runs away, makes the stallion chase her."

"Yes." His voice had fallen to its deeper, more intimate timbre. "But they both know that it's only a game, part of the courting ritual. That eventually they'll end up together."

She didn't answer that. She couldn't. If she turned to face him, she might very well find herself in his arms. And here, behind the chutes, was not a good place for an embrace.

She moved around the mare, finishing the routine without conscious thought. Her mind was racing. Surely Alex's words meant more than they actually said. If he were the palomino stallion, she was surely the little dark mare. And she didn't think she could run very far, if at all.

Giving Gypsy a pat on the nose, she moved off to stow her tack. Her hands were trembling slightly; she hoped he wouldn't notice. She fed and watered the horse while Alex stood patiently, a contented smile on his face.

Finally she was done. Unless she wanted to start rearranging the straw on the stall floor there was nothing more to do. She looked toward him.

He came instantly alert. "All done?"

"Yes."

"Where's your room?"

Her heart leaped to her throat, threatened to choke her. "Motel," she said, waving a hand. "Over there."

He grinned. "Mine, too."

Only then did she realize what she had let him know—that she meant to stay the night in Miles City.

"What do you say we wash up and have a leisurely dinner? I hear there's a pretty good steak house in these parts."

"Sounds good." Her heart was behaving more sensibly now. She hoped she hadn't given herself away by her reaction to that question about the room. She should have known that Alex was not the kind to bluntly ask "Your room or mine?" It was her own fault, of course, for letting her mind dwell on his kisses and the feel of his body against hers.

He took her hand and a shiver went up her spine as he led her toward the gate. "Are you a fast dresser?" he asked, his eyes dancing.

Her lips curved automatically into an answering smile. "Give me half an hour. Is that fast enough?"

"I think so." His fingers squeezed hers. "But no longer," he warned, his smile belying the intensity of his tone. "Because I'm starving."

8

·◦◦◦◦◦◦◦◦◦·

It took Emily exactly twenty-seven minutes to strip off her dirty clothes, shower and wash her hair and slip into the only dress she had with her. A gauze peasant-type dress, it picked up the blue in her eyes. She shook out the skirt, thankful that gauze was supposed to look wrinkled, and ran the brush through her damp curls. As usual, they tumbled riotously, but they would dry quickly. It was an easy style for someone who shampooed every day. That was why she had chosen it.

She picked up her lipstick, put a soft touch of coral to her mouth. An even softer touch of blue-green eye shadow tinted her eyelids. And that completed her makeup. No foundation, no powder, no mascara. Just her own fresh complexion.

Turning away from the mirror, she slid her feet into narrow-strapped sandals and glanced down at her watch. Exactly thirty minutes had passed since Alex had left her at her door.

A soft tap sounded on that door and she smiled. He was very punctual. She turned to open it.

"Wow!" The word was spoken quietly, almost reverently. And its import could not be mistaken. Alex was impressed with what he saw. Very impressed.

For her part, Emily found him impressive, too. His dark suit contrasted with a white shirt. Only three things differentiated him from an eastern business-man. His string tie, his cowboy boots and the Stetson he was twirling in his hands.

"Right on the dot," Emily said. "You're very punctual."

He grinned. "You, too. But *I* should be compliment-ing *you*. It's the woman who always keeps the man waiting. Oops!" He had caught the look on her face and realized his error. "A sexist statement if I *ever* heard one. I apologize."

"Apology accepted," she replied as she turned to pick up her purse and shawl. "I'm ready."

As they made their way down the hall, Alex reached for her hand, tucking it through his arm with a smile that would have melted the coldest heart. Her fingers seemed to tingle as they met his coat sleeve and she felt the warmth of his arm beneath.

He didn't say much as he helped her into his car and set out toward the restaurant. She was conscious of several feelings: excitement, joy at being with him, a touch of fear and a nagging sense of having let Cherry down. The latter was made worse by the carping part of her mind that always blamed her for any failure and this time insisted caustically that she had let Cherry down because of a man.

She tried to defend herself from this unfair attack. But there was some truth in it. She *had* been thinking of Alex just before the event. How could she be *sure* that it was the calf's swerving and not her inattention that had made the loop miss?

The steak house was not far from the motel, and seeing the line of people Emily resigned herself to a long wait. To her surprise, however, Alex took her elbow and propelled her to the front. "Calloway," he said crisply. "We have reservations."

"Right this way, Mr. Calloway."

A slightly dazed Emily followed the hostess to a table. He grinned at her as he pulled out her chair. "Something wrong? You look surprised."

"The reservations . . ."

"Oh, I made those the first thing I got here. That's the reason for the fast dressing."

She nodded. "Are you always so well organized?"

"Usually. A man in my business can't afford to stand around in lines. Besides, if I'm meeting someone to interview it always looks better to have clout."

She managed a small smile, but the nagging voice in her mind persisted. You let Cherry down because of a man. And now you're sitting here enjoying yourself.

She felt a sense of melancholy settling over her as she tried to concentrate on the menu.

"How do you like your steak done?" Alex asked.

"Medium-rare," she answered automatically, still fighting the voice in her head.

His eyes seemed to hold a question, but he didn't say any more until the waiter had gone with their orders. Then he turned to her, his face serious. "Something's wrong, Emily. What is it?"

She hesitated. How could she explain this to a man? But the need to talk was so strong. And if any man could understand, it was Alex. She took a deep breath. "It's that first go-round. When I missed the calf."

"Yes?" His full attention was focused on her, but it didn't make her uncomfortable.

"I feel bad that I missed the calf."

He nodded. "I guess that's natural."

"I suppose so. But . . ." She didn't quite know how to say it. "I was thinking about something else . . . just before the event. Something that might have spoiled my concentration."

His eyes bored into hers, but all he said was, "The throw looked real good to me. The calf just swerved."

"That's what I've been telling myself." She looked down at her hands, not really seeing them. "But the fact is that I missed. And that cost Cherry prize money."

"Then you won your event. And that makes you feel doubly guilty. Right?"

She looked up at him in surprise. Understanding she had expected from him. But this kind of insight . . . "Yes, that's it. My mistake hurt Cherry a lot more than it hurt me."

He nodded. "And this, whatever it was, that you were thinking about before the event, is it connected to your guilt, too?"

She stared at him. "How did you know?"

His smile was tender. "Remember my sisters? I know something of how women think. Was it me you were thinking of?"

She knew lying was impossible, the truth was already written on her face. "Yes," she murmured.

"So," he went on. "You feel that you let Cherry down, that you made your 'mistake' because of a man." His smile was compassionate. "That's a kind of betrayal, isn't it? To let your friend down because of a man?"

She nodded again, unable to speak because of the tears gathering in her eyes. He had analyzed her feelings exactly, understood the whole thing.

"There's not much I can say to that," he went on softly. "Your feelings are your own responsibility. I can't do anything about them. Oh, I can suggest—or even insist—that your throw was perfect. But that really won't do any good. Not if *you* don't believe it."

He looked up as the waiter approached with their salads. "I rest my case," he said, giving her a smile.

The tears had slowly receded, giving her a chance to speak. "Did you ever consider being a lawyer?" she asked, her voice light.

His smile showed relief. "Nope. My love of words doesn't extend that far." His voice deepened and grew gentle. "I have selfish reasons, too," he said, "for wanting this to be a special evening. I'm sure you're not unaware of them."

There was that look again, that promise that warmed her blood and made her breath quicken. And she knew suddenly, surely, that Cherry, if she knew about this, would not want her to turn her back on Alex, on what he was offering her. For Cherry was, above all things, a lively, loving young woman.

Emily smiled suddenly as she recalled Cherry's earlier encouraging words about Alex. Cherry, with her unbounded enthusiasm, would undoubtedly grin and say, "Go for it, Em. Give it all you've got."

Cherry was not against men, in spite of the way some of them acted. And she was certainly not against love.

Emily took up her fork and attacked her salad with a

will. She had suddenly realized just how hungry she was, how long it had been since breakfast.

She threw a glance at Alex and found him looking at her. "I feel better now," she said. "Thank you."

He shrugged his dark-clad shoulders. "You're welcome, I'm sure. But all I really did was listen."

She knew he had done more than that. And so did he. But she did not contradict him. "Listening can be very useful, too," she said. "Most people don't really listen. They just wait until they can take over the conversation."

His grin was boyish. "I'm glad you said 'people' instead of 'men.'"

It was her turn to shrug. "Women can be just as bad about that as men." She grinned at him. "The double standard shouldn't hold for anything," she continued. "For instance, they say women do a lot of gossiping, that they can't keep secrets." The thought of the plan made her momentarily proud. "But I've seen men . . . My brothers are the biggest gossips around. They can give you the details of the love life of every cowboy in the state."

At his look of amazement, she chuckled. "Well, maybe not *every* one, but a great many. And as for secrets . . ." She shook her head. "It's common knowledge that if you want the whole rodeo circuit to know something in a hurry, you tell it to Ted or Joe. The next day everyone in Montana will know it."

Alex had finished his salad and was regarding her over the rim of his coffee cup. "Your eyes sparkle when you're angry," he said softly, in that low, intimate tone that made her tremble. But he had no time to add more, for the waiter appeared with the rest of their dinners.

Emily dug in right away, aware that the salad had stimulated rather than dulled her appetite. The steak was heavenly, cooked just right. And she told Alex so some minutes later as she shoved her empty plate aside and leaned back. "I am stuffed," she added, her voice full of contentment.

"Good. I bet you skipped lunch."

She nodded. "I can't compete with food in my stomach. It interferes with my concentration." She looked at her empty plate. "I've got to admit I was really hungry. That hit the spot."

"Good. Do you want something for your sweet tooth? Some dessert?"

She sighed. "No, thanks. I'm not sure I can get out of the chair now."

"Maybe I should carry you." He eyed her figure, which in spite of the heavy meal, was slender and boyish.

Her laughter sounded nervously in her ears and she realized that she was, indeed, nervous. No man had ever affected her in this way. She didn't quite know how to behave, how to react to him.

He pushed back his chair. "How about a ride? A moonlight look at the prairie?"

"That sounds good." Again she felt afraid to look at him. What if he could read the desire in her eyes as plainly as she could read it in his?

His hand was warm on her bare elbow as he helped her into the car. He was silent as he climbed into the driver's seat and eased out of the parking lot.

She could feel her heart pounding under the thin cotton dress, pounding in a way it never had for Jerry Graves—or any other man.

He drove silently for about ten minutes, until the lights of the town had vanished behind them. Only the headlights of the car revealed the road and the soft glow of moonlight over the dusky prairie grass. It was beautiful, she thought. Beautiful and mysterious.

She tried to think of something to say, anything to break the tension between them. But everything she considered seemed inane and stupid. She could only think of the touch of his lips on hers, the feel of his arms around her. And the fact that the prairie was lonely and deserted.

He turned to her suddenly, his eyes leaving the road for a second. "Beautiful, isn't it?"

"Yes." She was grateful that he had said something. "I've always loved it, especially at night. There's something mysterious about it in the dark."

"I know." He turned the car over a cattle guard and up a narrow road toward a clump of cottonwoods silhouetted against the horizon. "I found this spot today," he said. "I thought . . . I hoped . . . maybe we'd come here tonight." His voice dropped and her body trembled at the note of intimacy that it held. "We watched the daylight sky together." She remembered his kisses as vividly as if they had occurred only moments before. "And I thought it would be nice to look at the nighttime sky, too."

She managed to nod, managed even to add, "The sky is usually very clear, so the stars are easy to see."

"I'm pretty sure we're going to see stars," he replied and she heard the laughter in his voice. But they had reached the clump of trees and he braked the car to a stop.

She didn't wait for him to help her out, but opened the door and stood waiting while he took something from behind his seat. Then he was beside her, taking her hand and leading her toward the little stream that glittered in the moonlight.

As they paused on its bank, she drew in her breath. Alex dropped the pile of things he was carrying, chose a blanket and spread it out. "No peanut butter and jelly sandwiches this time," he said lightly.

She nodded. "I guess we'll have to act like grown-ups."

He eyed the water speculatively. "I don't know. That water looks real inviting."

She gasped as the full import of his words struck her. "Alex!"

"Your brothers aren't around," he said in his most reasonable voice. "There's not a house in sight. The main road is more than five minutes back that way. And we can see anyone coming in plenty of time. Their lights would warn us. To say nothing of the sound of a motor."

"I . . . I . . ." She knew suddenly that she wanted to do this crazy thing, impossible as it seemed.

"Come on," he urged. "I'll beat you in."

She was lost then, her common sense vanquished by the sight of him shedding his clothes. Her own hands moved swiftly and they finished at the same time and stood, frozen for a moment in time, their eyes full of each other. Then the moment was gone and he grabbed her hand and pulled her into the water.

It was not a large stream, only knee-deep, but to her it was beautiful, a fairy-tale setting.

When he reached the center he dropped her hand and turned to splash her. She gasped as cool water hit warm flesh, and retaliated immediately, throwing handfuls of water on his bare chest.

It was a very masculine chest, she noted. Muscular and strong, with a fine coating of golden hair that caught the drops of water and held them like precious, shimmering jewels.

He threw great handfuls of water at her; then, not content with that, he grabbed her hand and threw himself down. As he pulled at her, she lost her balance and fell against him, her body sliding and slipping against his, making desire flame up in her so that even in the cool water her flesh felt hot.

His arms went around her, pulling her close against him. She felt the warmth of his body, the maleness of him. She wanted him, she wanted him so much. And he wanted her. His lips were wet against hers. She tasted the clear stream water on them as his hands slid over her back, down to her bare bottom.

Then suddenly they were submerged, their mouths still locked. She felt the sandy bottom of the stream against her hip as he rolled them over and pulled her to her knees.

As he knelt there facing her, his eyes filled with adoration, he reached out a tentative hand to touch her breast, gleaming white in the moonlight. "So beautiful," he whispered. "You're so beautiful. A nymph risen from the water to torment men."

"Torment?" Her protest was made softly, but she knew he understood it. If there were any tormenting being done, he was doing his share of it, kneeling there so virile and masculine, with the moonlight glinting on his body.

"Okay," he whispered. "No chauvinist remarks."

He bent suddenly to take a dusky nipple in his mouth. A little moan escaped from her lips and she swayed toward him, her hands going out to his shoulders for support.

She didn't quite know how it happened, but suddenly they were kneeling knee to knee, their naked bodies pressed together. Her arms went around his neck, his around her waist, as his lips devoured hers.

When he released her mouth, he kept her body close. His lips against her ear, he whispered hoarsely, "Emily, I want you. I want you so much."

She wanted to tell him that she wanted him, that she'd been longing for this moment, too, but all she could do was mutter an almost incoherent, "Yes, oh, yes."

That was all he needed, for he got to his feet and helped her to hers, pulling her again into his arms. So conscious was she of the feel of his body against hers that she could think of nothing else. Then suddenly he scooped her up into his arms. Her arms went automatically around his neck, as though they belonged there, she thought happily. Then she had to shut her mind to the pain that followed that thought. There might only be this one night, this one magic night.

Well, she had faced that. And she would handle it. Better one night with Alex than a lifetime with Jerry Graves. She banished thought, then, and gave herself up to sensation, to the warm strength of the arms that held her, to the slippery feel of her breasts against his chest.

He stepped easily out of the stream and up onto the blanket, where he set her on her feet. "So beautiful," he said again, drawing her down beside him on the blanket. His lips, moving eagerly over her wet body, left behind a trail of quivering warmth. She tried to pull him down against her, but he resisted her grasping hands and continued to shower kisses on her.

Her body was going wild. She ached deep inside, an ache that only he could stop. "Oh, Alex," she moaned, but his hands continued their exploration of her body and his mouth followed, driving her further into a sweet, sweet longing. It was almost as though she had waited all her life for this, she thought, as her hands plucked futilely at his shoulders, as her body arched upward toward his. This was a part of herself she had never known existed, this terrible, primeval need deep within her, a need so strong that it drove all sensible thought away.

Nothing seemed to matter except the feel of his body against hers. She had not forgotten that his stay in Montana was temporary, that he would soon be moving on. She knew quite well that this might be their only night together. But in the face of the feelings that overwhelmed her everything else paled to insignificance. She simply couldn't care: all her thoughts, all her feelings, were centered on the moment, on the man she had wanted so much and the wonderful things he was doing to her.

She cried out as his questing fingers reached the core of her being. "Oh, Alex, please!" She hardly recognized her own voice, deepened and made breathless by passion.

"Yes, yes," he murmured, shifting his body so that it was aligned above hers, but not touching it. The moon went behind a cloud and she could see only his outline, the hard male shape of him, and the longing within her grew and grew.

Finally, when she thought he would never touch her, he lowered himself gently. A sigh of contentment issued from her depths as she felt him against her. But contentment changed instantly to desire as she opened herself to him. This was how it was supposed to be, she thought, her arms going around his neck as his lips sought hers. No questions. No promises. Just the two of them united. Just the moment.

His lips left hers and he buried his face in her shoulder. Her body arched upward against his, wanting, needing. Her hands moved on his back, feeling the hard muscles of his shoulders. She wished she could keep the moment forever in memory. Everything about it—from the feel of his body against her own to the sweet smell of the prairie grass and the soft chirping of the crickets.

Then he began to move against her. Slowly at first, then faster and faster. Her breath came in great gasps and her body moved in time with his, while great surges of feeling rolled over her trembling flesh and a storm of ecstasy gathered deep within her. It broke finally, that storm, like a great cloud opening and deluging her with pleasure so intense that for a moment she hung on the edge of unconsciousness.

Her own cries echoed faintly through her head, as his hoarse breathing exploded against her neck and she knew that he had joined her in ecstasy.

Their bodies still joined, they lay for several minutes, regaining their breath. Then Alex rolled onto his back and pulled her against his side. "Now," he said, and the laughter was back in his voice, "let's look at the stars *up there.*"

9

The morning sun was bright on her closed eyelids and Emily stirred, twisting her head away. The movement brought her closer to consciousness and she realized abruptly that she was not alone in the bed. A warm male body was pressed against her back and a strong hand was cupped around one breast.

She snuggled back against him and wondered if Alex were awake. His hand didn't move so she lay still, letting her mind drift back to the night before and how wonderful it had been.

They had lain there for some time, watching the stars, their satisfied bodies still intertwined. She had not known a man could be so gentle and yet so masculine. He had touched her there in the starlight, kissed her and caressed her until she had wanted him again. And the second time had been even better than the first.

And then he had said, his lips soft against her ear, "Would you like to go back to the motel now? To the same room?"

"Yes." She had no false modesty. And so they had returned to her room. And it had been almost dawn before their longing for each other had been sated and they'd fallen asleep, their bodies comfortably touching.

But now she could feel her nipple rising under his hand and she moved slightly so she could look at her watch. It was midmorning.

Her movement roused him and his fingers tightened on her breast as his lips moved on the nape of her neck. "Good morning," he said softly. "Or is it afternoon?"

"Not yet," she replied, rolling over toward him, wanting to feel her breasts against his chest, the long, hard length of his body against hers.

They lay on their sides, facing each other, their bodies touching slightly. He smiled at her. "Last night was perfect," he said. "Just perfect. Thank you."

"Thank you," she replied, fighting her rising desire. "It was perfect for me, too."

He chuckled as his hands moved over her back. Familiar hands now. There was not an inch of her body that he had failed to explore, to delight in. He probably knew it better than she did herself, she thought, stirring against him as she asked, "What's so funny?"

"Us."

"Why?"

"Well, we've kind of agreed that we took a lot of our views of life from the movies, however idealistic they may be."

"Yes," she murmured, more interested in the body against her own than in his words.

"Well, it just occurred to me that the movies didn't give us any help for last night. But we did very well anyway."

A giggle started deep inside her and worked its way upward in a bubble of laughter. "Alan Ladd—or Shane—couldn't have done it better," she agreed.

He squeezed her then till she squealed for air. "Maybe we didn't need the movies after all," he said solemnly. "Maybe reality is better than we thought."

She knew he was joking—at least halfway—and she kept her voice light as she replied, "It is today."

That was all she asked for, she told herself. She'd had last night. This morning was a bonus, a gift.

"When do you have to leave for home?" he asked, his lips against her neck.

"I told Mom I was going to stay over and do some shopping. She won't expect me till late."

"What about Gypsy?" he said. "Will she need to be cared for?"

"There's a boy who takes care of any horses that are still here."

"Then we can have the whole day."

Regret hit her, and dismay. "I . . . I can't," she said. "I . . . I have to go to a meeting at one o'clock. It's . . ." She cast around in her mind for a suitable excuse. "It's about some rodeo rules we want changed." That wasn't a lie, exactly. After all, they did want things changed.

His hand moved on her body and desire leaped in her. "And you *have* to be there."

She hesitated. It must sound strange to him. She wished she could tell him the truth. He wasn't like the others: he would understand. But it wasn't her secret, she reminded herself.

"It's the old loyalty bit, isn't it," he whispered, his mouth moving to her breast. "You can't let your friends down."

Her breath was coming faster now, so the little gasp she gave might have come from his touch. But it was his ability to understand her, to know what was going on in her mind, that had startled her again. It was almost as though he could think like a woman. "Yes," she admitted. "I have to be there. I promised."

He raised a hand to look at his own watch. "I have ten-thirty. And, since you're a fast dresser, half an hour is plenty of time for that. So, that gives us two hours."

His fingers hadn't quit moving as he talked, teasing fingers that knew all the right places to touch, that knew how to do wonderful things to her exultant body.

"Two hours," she repeated lazily, her hands moving across his back and down to his narrow waist.

"Yes." He kissed the tip of her nose. "Now the question arises. How do we spend those two hours?" He kissed her eyelids and the point of her chin.

"We could have a leisurely breakfast and do a little shopping," she teased, trying to sound serious.

"That's option number one." He nodded. "We could have a quick breakfast and come back to bed. Option number two." He grinned as he crushed her tightly to him. "Or, option number three, we could skip breakfast altogether and find out if we can see stars in the daylight. Which do you prefer?"

With her face buried in his neck, she felt her blood pounding. She was totally aware of her body, every demanding cell of it. And food was the furthest thing from her thoughts. Still . . . "If you're hungry," she began.

"Hey, what is this?" He pulled the upper part of his body back until he could see her face. "I thought you were a liberated woman."

She stared at him. "Whatever are you talking about?"

"I asked you what *you* wanted," he said. "Can the stuff about if *I'm* hungry. What do *you* want?"

Her heart threatened to flip over in her breast. I want you, she wanted to scream. I want you for the rest of my life. For one wild moment she thought she'd said the words aloud, but his expression didn't change and she swallowed a sigh of relief. Later she would think of what she'd just discovered. But now he was waiting for an answer, his eyes bright.

She moistened her lips. "I . . . I'm not very hungry," she said. When he didn't reply, but continued to stare at her, she floundered on. "I'll be having lunch with the girls. But you—"

His mouth cut off the rest of her words and she gave herself up to his kiss, losing herself in the emotions it aroused.

When he drew back, he was smiling. "If we're going to get rid of the double standard," he said, "you've got to do your share. No more expecting the man to make all the advances. No more expecting the woman to go along with whatever he wants. Agreed?"

"Agreed."

"Good. Now, how about a straight answer? Do you want to make love or do you want to eat breakfast?" His eyes danced. "First."

Her laughter bubbled up again. "I want to make

117

love," she said, surprised at how easy it was. "And I want to do it now." And suiting her actions to her words, she got to her knees and began covering his chest with little kisses.

"See?" he said triumphantly. "It isn't hard at all."

Her mouth busy, she nodded. It might not be hard, she thought, to tell him that she wanted to make love. But to be completely honest—to tell him that she wanted their relationship to last, that the thought of marriage had entered her mind—that she could never do. The double standard might be weakening, she thought, but women still did not do the proposing.

Then she pushed such thoughts from her mind and concentrated on the present. Here lay Alex, the most attractive man she had ever met, his hard masculine body hers to explore. Tentatively, for she had little experience at this sort of thing, she began to caress him.

She let herself be guided by his sounds of pleasure, realizing quickly how they fueled her own desire, how the feel of his flesh against her lips, against her sensitive fingertips, fed that desire.

Finally he groaned and rolled over, pinning her to the bed. "My God," he panted. "You could drive a man crazy like that."

She moved against him, her lips against his neck. "Or a woman."

"Or a woman," he agreed before his mouth covered hers. Then they were joined and there was no more talking. Only the sound of their labored breathing until joy hit them both at the same moment and swept them up in timeless bliss.

Later, after their breathing had slowed to normal, Alex raised himself and looked at his watch. "Still time for breakfast," he said, his eyes dancing.

"What do *you* want?" she asked, trying to make her question an imitation of his earlier one.

His eyes burned into hers and her sated body leaped to life again. "I want you," he said. "Again and again and again."

When she entered the private dining room at five after one, Emily wondered how she looked. She'd cut her dressing time to fifteen minutes by not washing her hair and then wasted several minutes staring at herself in the mirror. She not only felt different, she looked different. There was a softness to her face, a kind of glow.

Now, moving toward the table where her friends were gathered, she could still feel Alex's arms around her, his good-bye kiss. His parting words rang in her ears. "I've got to hit a couple rodeos. I have some interviews set up. But I should be back at the ranch in a couple of days." He had added nothing to that, no words of love or of promise. But there had been that promise in his eyes. At least he was coming back. For the moment that was enough. It had to be.

Cherry looked up as she reached the table. "Hi, Em." She looked as though she were about to add something else, then thought better of it.

"Hi, Emily. Sit down. We've been waiting for you."

Pulling out a chair, Emily took her place at the table. "Sorry I'm late. I got busy and forgot the time."

Cherry's eyes danced at this and Emily wondered if her friend could have found out about Alex, about last night. But probably she was just guessing.

"Let's eat first," said Marilyn, a petite blonde whose face was liberally sprinkled with freckles. "Then we can talk."

Everyone agreed to this and soon they were all

busy with their food. She was very hungry, Emily discovered suddenly, digging into the food and trying to focus her thoughts on the meeting ahead. But they would not be diverted and while she ate her mind replayed the events of the past night.

Finally everyone was finished and the empty plates were removed. "Now," Marilyn said. "Let's get down to business." She glanced at a woman to her right. In surprise, Emily realized that she didn't know this woman. Marilyn had brought a newcomer to the meeting and she had been so engrossed in thoughts of Alex that she hadn't even noticed.

"This is Liz McGuire," Marilyn told Emily, responding to her friend's curious look. "She's a reporter."

Emily stirred uncomfortably. It seemed early to be involving the press. From their worried expressions it was clear that several of the others thought the same.

"Liz is my cousin's sister-in-law," Marilyn went on. "We can trust her. And"—she paused dramatically—"she works for one of the Vegas papers."

A murmur of excitement raced around the table.

The newspaperwoman nodded. "I give you my word. Nothing leaks out. Nothing. Now give me the lowdown."

Marilyn glanced around the table. The assembled women nodded in agreement. Emily, her fears assuaged, did the same.

Marilyn continued. "Emily applied to the PRCA for a permit as E. M. Asperson. We plan to have her compete at the Elks Helldorado in Vegas. We wanted a big-money event, where we can really prove our point. Of course, as you know, the best-paying rodeos are by invitation or for top competitors."

Liz looked surprised. "She's not going to barrel race?"

Marilyn laughed. "No, she's entering the calf roping."

"But that's only for men." Liz looked confused.

"We know. E. M. *is* a man. At least, to the PRCA."

"Has she competed as a man before?" the reporter
asked.

Marilyn shook her head. "No."

Liz eyed her speculatively. "She looks awfully
small."

Marilyn shook her head. "Em's the best we've got.
We all agreed on that." She smiled. "We believe in
her. So much so that we raised the thousand dollars to
get the permit and the extra for entry money."

"Then you'll split the prize money," Liz said. "But I
don't see why you need me."

Marilyn shook her head. "But we do. After Em
wins, she's going to talk to you, and the other
reporters. To tell them she's a woman."

"But you'll lose the prize money that way."

Marilyn shrugged disdainfully. "We know that.
We're not after the money. We're looking to prove
something. That women can compete with men and
win."

"And if she doesn't win?" Liz was clearly skeptical.

"If she gets a good time, that'll do almost as well,"
Cherry said. "But I know Em. She'll win, won't you?"

"I'll do my best." The memory of that lost loop rose
up to haunt her, but Cherry's clear eyes held only
admiration and belief. She was a true friend. "I'll do
my very best," Emily repeated.

The reporter looked around the table, silently
counting. "Ten of you," she said. "That's a hundred
apiece."

"Plus entry money," Cherry reminded her. "But
it's for a good cause. A real good cause. We're sick

and tired of being treated like babies. We want to prove we're as good as the men." She giggled. "At least, Em is."

A chuckle of agreement went up from the others.

"You're all capable of competing with men," Emily said. She turned to the reporter. "We don't expect to be able to change the rules," she explained, liking the understanding she saw in the reporter's dark eyes. "At least not yet. But we're tired of being lorded over and pushed around."

"Yeah," Cherry said. "Why, just today I heard an official scold Helen for saying a four-letter word—" She grinned. "Not the worst one, either—when her bronc tried to smash her leg against the chute. A cowboy wouldn't have stopped with one four-letter word. We all know that."

"And no official would have scolded him, either," Marilyn added.

"And did you hear," asked Cathy, whose blond hair and freckles were almost identical to her sister's, "how he gave all the credit for Em's winning to her daddy?"

Cherry's usually pleasant face was distorted by anger. "I can sure think of some unladylike words to apply to him."

Liz looked around the table. "I don't know much about rodeoing," she said slowly. "I'm a city girl myself. So let me ask some questions now. It'll help with the story later. That is, if there is a story."

"There will be," Marilyn said quietly. "We're sure of it."

Emily wished that she had Marilyn's confidence. Ever since she'd met Alex her own seemed to have failed her.

"So you're telling me"—Liz McGuire's voice broke

into her thoughts—"that the men laugh at women's rodeo."

"We just lately got the name changed from 'all-girl rodeo,'" one commented.

Liz went on. "That the prize money is small. No big sponsors, et cetera. That the announcers and officials are sexist."

Heads were nodding vigorously around the table. "You can't have saddle bronc or steer wrestling events. And you just feel discriminated against all around."

Again heads nodded. "Well, that seems pretty clear. And pretty lousy. I guess that's par for the course." A sudden bitter grin curved the newspaperwoman's lips. "But things are looking up for us. Not too many years ago I couldn't have covered the rodeo. Or if I had, it would have been to look at fashion."

A moan went up from the women.

"That's another thing," Cathy added. "We have to dress properly. Look feminine." She snorted. "And that ain't easy."

Liz nodded. "Now, tell me exactly what you want from me."

Emily leaned forward with the rest. The door to the private dining room was closed, but still Marilyn lowered her voice. "If . . . *when* Em wins," she corrected herself, "she'll tell the officials the truth. We want to make sure they don't cover it up. We want to get national coverage. If we can."

Liz nodded thoughtfully. "I think I can help there. I've got a friend at *Time*."

"Great." Marilyn's eyes shone. "Now, can you be there, with a photographer, when Em spills the beans?"

"There'll be a lot of reporters there," Liz said. "I

don't see how they can shut them all up." She eyed Emily critically. "I'm just not sure it'll get that far. You don't look anything like a man to me."

Emily felt the blush rising to her cheeks. It was her lovemaking with Alex that had left her feeling soft and womanly. And it did show. "Lots of men have curly hair," she said. "I'll wear bulky clothes. And I'll keep my hat jammed down. They just won't be expecting a woman."

The reporter still didn't seem satisfied, but all she said was, "It's a long shot. But I guess it's worth a try."

As the others gathered around and began to offer still more information, Emily again lost track of the conversation. The reporter's words had shocked her. Until now, she hadn't thought beyond the actual competition. Oh, she'd known the plan, but she hadn't envisioned anything beyond the roping event. She certainly hadn't imagined herself facing a horde of disbelieving reporters, of having to prove her female-ness or answer probing questions. And even worse, she thought suddenly, would be having to go home afterward, to face the derision and disgust of her brothers. Her father might give her grudging respect, but Ted and Joe, no matter how she might succeed, would never give her that. They would always find some way to denigrate her accomplishments. She felt a heavy weight of sadness settling over her. How could men ever be persuaded to see things differently? Her brothers, Jerry Graves, all the men in Jordan, even her own father, who gave her some emotional support in competition . . . None of them could un-derstand what seemed so clear to the women gathered at this table.

None of them was willing—"dared" was the right word—to meet a woman as an equal. That was the core of it, she decided with a sigh. It was almost as though these men had to see women as inferior in order to keep their masculinity. All the men she knew were like that. All except Alex.

Would he understand? she wondered. Would he be proud of her for taking this stand? For showing the world what a woman could do? Somehow, she felt he would. That he was on her side.

With a start, she realized that the women around her were pushing back their chairs. The meeting was over. Stifling a sigh, she joined Cherry for the walk back to the barns. She only hoped she hadn't promised more than she could deliver.

10

~**oooooooooo**~

When Emily arrived at the ranch late that evening, she was thankful to find her mother alone. She felt bone-tired and she certainly didn't need any of the habitual hazing that her brothers loved to dish out.

Noreen Asperson looked up from the sink where she was washing lettuce for a salad. "Hi, honey. How did it go?"

Emily managed a smile. "Not too bad, Mom. I won the calf roping event. Messed up on the team thing, though. Darn calf turned his head at the last second and I missed him. Had to use my backup rope. And you know what that means."

Her mother nodded, pushing at hair just a shade lighter than Emily's. "Was Cherry upset?"

"No. You know how good she is. She blamed the calf." Emily sank into a chair and sighed.

"But you blame yourself."

It wasn't a question and Emily didn't treat it like one.

"I just don't know, Mom. I thought the loop was good. It looked like it would fall just right. And then it didn't."

"The past is over," her mother said, putting the bowl of salad on the table. "Just let it go. I've got fresh biscuits in the oven. And stuffed pork chops."

"Are the boys coming?" Emily got to her feet and moved toward the cupboard. "Shall I set places for them?"

"No. Not for your father, either. He's over in Brockway, looking at some stock. So there's just the two of us. Unless Mr. Calloway gets back."

Her searching look wasn't lost on Emily, but somehow Emily couldn't bring herself to talk about Alex. "You mean you made stuffed pork chops and biscuits? Just for me?"

She took down the plates and cups, opened the drawer to get out the silver. "That was real nice of you, Mama." The childish name slipped out before she was aware of it. How nice it would be, she thought wistfully, if she could go back to the old days when Mama had had the answer for every childish question, the solution to every problem. But those days were gone. They would never return. She was a grown woman, an adult, and she had to solve her own problems, difficult as that might seem.

"Get your shopping done?" her mother asked, startling her so that a cup rattled perilously against a saucer and almost fell.

"Ah, no. I slept late." She turned away so her blush wouldn't show. "Then the girls got together for lunch. By the time that was over I just wanted to get home."

"I understand," her mother replied softly, setting boiled potatoes and corn on the table.

Emily busied herself pouring the coffee. There was something in her mother's expression, in the tone of her voice, that told her daughter that she did indeed understand. Everything.

Was it really possible? Emily wondered. Could her face have given her away? Mothers were supposed to know about things like that.

She pulled her chair up to the laden table. "Everything smells great. You shouldn't work so hard just for me."

"Hey!" Her mother took the chair nearest the stove, the seat from which she inevitably rose a dozen times a meal to refill bowls or glasses, to get some requested item that no one ever thought of going after himself. "Women deserve good meals, too, you know."

The pork chops were delicious, the stuffing even more so and the biscuits were the finishing touch. Fifteen minutes later, Emily polished off the last biscuit, pushed back her chair and clutched at her stomach. "I must have gained ten pounds," she moaned.

Her mother's smile was amused. "Nonsense. You work off everything you eat. You're like I was when I was young. I could eat anything and still stay slim."

Emily's expression sobered. "Have you ever been sorry?" she asked.

Her mother eyed her over her coffee cup. "For what?" she asked.

Emily's gesture was expansive. "Oh, for leaving the city. The kind of life you knew. For coming out here, away from everything. Away from your friends."

Her mother smiled, a smile that made the blue eyes so like Emily's own shine. "No. I've never regretted it. I hated the city. The crowds. The dirt. The impersonal feeling. When your father first brought me out here, I thought I'd discovered heaven."

She was quiet for a minute, evidently remembering. "It was lonely at first. But I had your father. And then your brothers. And finally you."

The words were softly spoken and revealed more than Noreen Asperson was aware of. Her daughter heard the years of loneliness, as well as the joy at having a daughter, another woman in the house.

"Mama, do you like Alex?" She felt the blood rising to her face. The moment of closeness had betrayed her into this confidence, but she desperately needed a woman to talk to and her mother was the only woman she could trust.

"Yes, I like him." Her mother's eyes were shrewd. "But that's not what's important. The important question is, Do *you* like him?"

Emily looked at her mother. "I think you know that I do." She stared thoughtfully into space. "He's different. He's gentle, tender. But he can be tough, too."

"He's not like your brothers," her mother agreed. "The West breeds hard men." She looked at her daughter closely. "They haven't entirely lost qualities like tenderness, but they're awfully good at hiding them."

"Joe and Ted . . ." Somehow she could never see her rowdy brothers caring, really caring about a woman.

Her mother laughed. "Even your brothers," she said. "All it takes is the right woman."

Emily shook her head. "I guess I'll have to take your word for it," she said finally. "But I just can't imagine it."

"What are you going to do about Alex?" her mother asked, bringing the conversation back to the subject.

Emily frowned. *"Do* about him?"

"Yes. Do you want him bad enough to fight for him, to give up roping, to follow him anywhere?"

Her mother's expression remained steady, but Emily caught the slight break in her voice at the thought of her daughter being far away. She shook her head. "I don't know. I don't know if there's anyone else to fight. I'd be giving up rodeo competition eventually anyway. Even the men don't stay in much after thirty. But I don't want to leave here."

She sighed. "Oh, Mama. In that respect he's just like the others. He's always going on down the road. He's a writer and writers travel a lot. They work in cities. You know how I hate cities. I need the sun and the land. I need my horses."

Her mother nodded. "I'm afraid there aren't any easy answers to these things. Only you can decide if he's worth sacrificing for."

Sudden temper flared in Emily's eyes and she pounded a fist on the table, rattling the empty dishes. "It's just not fair! Why should the woman have to do all the sacrificing? Why should we have to give up our homes and our careers? Why can't the men give sometimes?"

"Sometimes they do," her mother replied quietly. "Things are changing, honey. But that kind of change takes time. Lots of time." She sighed. "I wish I could be more help to you. But when I was growing up a normal woman had only one goal—a good marriage. If she made the right choice, she was supposed to live happily ever after." Her chuckle had a sad sound to it. "The fairy tale of the fifties. But we believed it."

For a moment they looked at each other in silence and Emily realized that her mother had not asked her if she loved Alex. Or if he loved her.

She smiled suddenly, sheepishly. "The truth of the matter is . . . I don't even know how Alex feels about me."

Her mother's eyes twinkled. "I think you've got a pretty good idea." She shifted her gaze, avoiding her daughter's eyes. "One thing I'm glad of. It's much easier to travel now than it used to be. If you move far away, you can at least get back to visit."

Emily pushed herself erect. "I think we're being kind of silly," she said with a soft laugh. "Alex Calloway is probably with a woman right now, enjoying himself."

Her mother looked at her sharply. "A man you can't trust isn't worth sacrificing for. No matter how attractive he is."

Emily began to gather up the dishes. "It isn't that, Mama. If we were married . . ." The words hung in the air between them. She clattered two plates together. "This is ridiculous. I've only known the man a week and I'm talking about marriage!"

Noreen Asperson shrugged as she rose and began to put away the leftovers. "It happens that way sometimes. You *have* heard of love at first sight," she added dryly.

"Yes, but—"

"I remember the first time I saw your father. He could hardly stand. His left arm was a bloody mess. And he was still grinning." She chuckled. "He even told me what pretty blue eyes I had. Before he passed out and I had to catch him."

The wistful look on her mother's face pulled at Emily's heartstrings. It seemed strange to think of her big hearty father as a wounded young soldier.

Her mother smiled. "I knew by the time I had his shirt cut off that he was the one. The right one for me." She reached under the sink for the dish soap. "You're the only one who can know, honey. You have to feel it inside." She smiled warmly. "I'd guess from the way you've been acting and talking, though, that this is it. But you're right." She turned the water on in the sink and reached for the dishcloth. "It is kind of early to be talking marriage."

Emily reached for a dish towel, but her mother motioned her away. "Go on now. You know drained dishes are more sanitary than wiped ones. The mail's in the office. Why don't you go sort it?"

"Okay. If you're sure."

"I'm sure. Now scat. This'll just take me a minute."

In the office Emily absently picked up the pile of mail and began to sort it into the various pigeonholes in the case her father had built. She stared at the labeled pigeonhole that bore Alex's name. Mr. Alex Calloway, she thought, then shook her head. Now she was behaving like a teenager, mooning around over some boy.

Her fingers moved slowly as she sorted the mail. There were always letters for Ted and Joe. A pink envelope caught her eye and she sniffed. The perfume it carried was not the subtlest. She shoved it in Ted's box. Another fan letter, no doubt. She smiled. The practice of announcing a cowboy's hometown gave the fans all the information they needed. The post office delivered a lot of letters bearing no more address than Ted Asperson, Jordan, Montana.

Her fingers paused and her heart thudded as her eyes fell on the next envelope, an envelope that bore Alex's name. At any other time she probably wouldn't have given it a second glance, but now, after the talk she'd just had with her mother, after Ted's pink perfumed fan letter, she couldn't help herself. Her eyes went automatically to the return address.

It was imprinted, giving an impression of wealth that the heavy, rich-textured gray envelope added to. Could Alex have a wealthy girlfriend in the East? Her heart thudded in her throat as she tried to pull her eyes away. But it was too late. The address printed there was already etched in her mind. Mrs. Harvey Wallace Livingstone III.

Her heart still thudding, Emily frowned. She had seen that name before. She was sure of it. She put the letter in Alex's box, barely stopping herself from sniffing it first, and continued to sort the rest of the mail.

Harvey Wallace Livingstone III. She had seen that name recently, read it someplace. A soft cry escaped her as she realized where. An article in *Time*, an article on rodeo. And Mrs. Harvey Wallace Livingstone III had been quoted. Emily could not remember exactly what she'd said.

She hurried to the bookshelves where the magazines were kept. It had been a very recent edition, either last week or the week before.

Ten minutes later she had found the article and stood staring at it in disbelief. Mrs. Livingstone was quoted all right. "Rodeo is a blood sport. Even more despicable than the bullfight. It maims animals with wanton cruelty, destroying hundreds and thousands every year. Such atrocities should be stopped immediately."

The magazine fell from Emily's lifeless fingers. What connection could Alex have with this Mrs. Livingstone? This couldn't be a simple letter of solicitation. Only his office had this address. Could Alex actually *know* this woman? Could they be—she tried to stop it, but her mind finished the thought—lovers?

The next two days were blurred for Emily. She tried to concentrate on the ranch, on her roping, on the plan. On anything but Alex and that terrible letter still in his box. But she couldn't get him out of her mind.

When she finally heard the car motor and saw the blue wagon coming up the drive, she was not sure how she felt. She wanted to see him, to be in his arms. But she was anxious and afraid. The import of that letter had grown to frightful proportions, grown more as each day passed. Now that she would have her answers, she was not at all sure she wanted them.

His face was wreathed in smiles as he came toward her. "Emily, how have you been?"

"Pretty good." She tried to keep her feelings off her face. This was not the place for confrontation. "How was your trip?"

"Great. I got some good stuff. But I was in a hurry to get back." His eyes lingered on hers and she felt her desire rising. "Could we take a ride?"

"Have you had lunch?" she asked. "We've eaten, but I can fix you something."

"I don't want lunch," he replied, his voice dropping to that intimate tone. "I want to get away from here so I can say hello properly."

I want that, too, she thought, but not until I know about that letter.

"Sure." She kept her voice calm and cheerful. "We can go for a ride. Meet you at the stables in ten minutes."

She hurried into the house to tell her mother. "Alex is back. We're going for a ride." Her mother made no reply, though her eyes were worried as they followed her out the door.

Perhaps she should have told her mother about that letter, Emily thought as she whistled to Gypsy. But how could she? It all seemed kind of silly. Except for Mrs. Livingstone's venomous words in *Time*. *They* were clear enough. She was out to get rodeo eliminated. She almost seemed to have a personal hatred for the sport. Certainly her words indicated a view somewhat less than objective.

Emily reached the stable just as Alex led out the saddled horses. "I couldn't wait," he said, his eyes dancing. "I'll put my stuff away later."

He offered her Gypsy's reins and she took them. "You have some mail," she said, watching his face.

He shrugged. "Let it wait." He swung up and grinned down at her. "Hurry up, slowpoke."

She managed a smile as she mounted. It was good to see him so anxious to be with her, but she couldn't fully feel her joy at seeing him again. The shadow of that letter lay between them. She would not be able to go into his arms until she knew what that woman meant to him. Swallowing a sigh, she turned Gypsy toward the prairie, heading for the spot where they had eaten their peanut butter and jelly lunch.

11

Half an hour later, the horses stood by the clump of cottonwoods. "Don't you know where there's an old line shack or a bunch of bushes or something?" Alex asked, turning to her with a gleam in his eyes.

She could not keep her body from responding to that look. "Farther upstream. There's an overhang with a little shelf underneath. It can't be seen unless you're right on it."

"Good. Let's go."

It took only a few minutes to reach the spot. Emily reined Gypsy in. "We'll leave the horses here."

He was there when she swung down, but she avoided his arms and, grabbing him by the hand, led him down a narrow path.

"Nice," he said, looking quickly around him.

Then she was in his arms. She didn't want to pull away, but she couldn't give herself fully to his kiss, not with that letter on her mind.

After a moment he released her. Taking her hand, he pulled her down on the little stretch of grass. "Okay. What is it? I thought you were just nervous, but something's definitely wrong."

Now that the moment was here she wished frantically that it wasn't. She was afraid to talk about it, yet she knew that some part of her was pleased at his sensitivity, pleased that he could tell when things were not right with her.

"I . . . I feel silly," she stammered.

"Whatever it is, let's get it over with," he said, his arm going around her shoulders. "I've been thinking about you all morning." He laughed. "Every time I started dictating I ended up with descriptions of you. So come on now. Get it over with." His eyes narrowed suddenly. "Did Graves come around? Have you been seeing him?"

"No, no. I haven't seen anyone." Was that relief in his eyes? Whatever it was, it gave her the courage to go on. "It's . . . it's that letter you got."

His eyes widened in surprise. "A letter? What letter?"

He didn't look guilty, she told herself. This Mrs. Livingstone couldn't mean anything to him. She took a deep breath. "It's . . . it's from Mrs. Harvey Wallace Livingstone the third," she went on. "I sort the mail, you see." She hurried on, wondering what he was thinking. But his face revealed nothing.

"So?"

"I . . ." She faltered. She couldn't tell him she was jealous. "I . . . I remembered her name." She laughed nervously. "It's an easy name to remember. She was quoted in *Time* last week." She looked at Alex but he remained silent, so she went on. "She said some terrible things about rodeo. I . . . I just wondered how you knew a person like that."

His eyes had clouded over; she could read nothing of his feelings there. "I met her at a cocktail party," he began and Emily's heart dropped. It was just as she had feared. They were lovers. "She's trying to get some kind of organization going to abolish rodeo. You know how the super-rich are. They have to have something to do."

Emily nodded. "Is she . . . very beautiful?"

For a minute he stared at her, then he burst into laughter.

She felt the tears rising. This was no laughing matter.

"So that's it," he said, squeezing her against him. When she tried to release herself, he just squeezed harder. "You're jealous."

She gasped. "I am not!" Her indignation was for his benefit. She couldn't hide the truth from herself, but she didn't intend to admit it to him. "I just thought it was strange. That you should know her."

"Writers know all kinds of people," he said, kissing the tip of her nose. "And for your information, Mrs. Harvey Wallace Livingstone the third is sixty-five years old, six feet tall and built like a barrel."

"Really?" It was absurd, she knew, yet she felt suddenly very lighthearted.

"Really. She reminds me of a talking bulldozer."

Emily laughed at the image, but the letter was still there. "But why would she be writing you?"

He shrugged, as well as he could with his arm around her. "She's been after me to join her group. The Society for the Abolition of Cruel and Inhumane Sports, I think it's presently called. She changes the name from time to time."

Emily digested this. "But how did she know to write you here?" she persisted. She felt better, but the whole thing still seemed strange.

Alex grinned at her. "It's clear you've never been rich," he said. "Mrs. Livingstone is an extremely persistent person, used to getting what she wants. Someone at the word processing office is probably a little richer for having leaked my address."

He brushed the matter aside with a gesture of his free hand. "I don't mind. Those girls aren't paid enough, anyway. I'll just pitch the letter."

"You're sure it was a girl?"

The glint in her eyes warned him and he chuckled. "Yes. I'm sure it was a *woman.*" His emphasis on the word told her he recognized his misuse of "girl." "Because, you sweet thing, all the people who work there, including the office manager, are women."

It was her turn to chuckle. "Okay. I concede." She lay back against his arm and turned her face to his. "So, how was your trip? Did your interviews go well?"

"Very well," he said. "Very well indeed. Except for one thing."

"And what was that?" She was conscious of the darkening of his eyes, the lowering of his voice, and her body responded.

"My mind kept going off on flights of fancy. Like in the movies when the shot shows the person's head and then fades into a scene that's all hazy around the edges."

"Uh-huh, go on."

"Well, imagine this. I'm sitting there, talking to this bull rider, see? And he's telling me how many ribs and other assorted bones he's broken this year, and I'm thinking about you and our night together. Suddenly he stops talking and I realize that he's been telling me how a bull stomped him and I'm sitting there with a silly smile on my face, nodding and saying, 'That's nice.'"

Laughter broke from her. "You didn't!"

"Yes, I did," he said. "And then I had to apologize. He was a nice guy, though. When I told him I was thinking about this woman I knew, he understood. And he told me I was lucky not to be competing, that thinking like that in the arena would get me stomped for sure. Then we finished the interview."

His fingers reached out to caress her cheek. "I guess it's a good thing I didn't have to do anything more dangerous than drive the car. 'Cause the truth is I've hardly thought of anything else since I left you the other morning."

"Me, too," she whispered just before his lips met hers, and she didn't feel the least bit of embarrassment for admitting it.

The little shelf of grass-covered earth was small, but it was big enough to accommodate two bodies, especially when they were so closely intertwined.

When Alex released her mouth, she sighed and snuggled closer to him. "This is nice," he said. "Very nice."

A soft giggle rose in her throat. "I found it when I was about ten. I used to pretend that I was surrounded by Indians. And I picked them off, one by one." She frowned. "I know now that the fighting was often the white man's fault. I wouldn't like someone coming in and ruining *my* country." She sighed. "Just think how beautiful this country used to be. Great herds of buffalo and wild horses running free. We spoiled it."

"In a way," he agreed. "Though there wouldn't have been any wild horses without the Spaniards. It's still very beautiful, though." He turned her face toward his. "Not as beautiful as you, of course." His fingers moved to her shirt, unbuttoning the front and pulling its tails out of her jeans.

She felt a thrill of fear. Not of Alex, but of making love in the daylight, out here on the prairie. But they really were safe, she told herself as he drew her shirt off. This little area was invisible from above because of the overhang and shielded from the creek by a screen of bushes. In all the years she had played here no one had ever disturbed her.

Alex's fingers had found the fastening on her bra, were pulling it off. Her flesh quivered as he touched it gently, reverently, and bent to plant a kiss on each rosy peak. She sighed again, this time in contentment.

"God, but you're beautiful," he said, in that deep voice that she so loved. "Just beautiful."

She made no answer to that; a thank-you seemed rather out of place. But she smiled at him, putting all her feeling into it. And her fingers moved to undo his shirt. She wanted to feel his chest against her bare breasts.

She was not as adept as he and she fumbled over a button. But he only smiled and leaned forward to kiss her forehead. Even that simple act sent a wave of feeling over her.

Finally she had his shirt open. Her hands went to the soft mat of chest hair, caressed the skin beneath it. He closed his eyes and his whisper barely reached her ears. "That feels so good."

Unable to wait any longer, she tugged off his shirt and put it aside, then went into his arms. The clink of metal startled them both and Alex laughed. "Belt buckles," he said. "But we'll soon fix that."

"In a minute," she whispered, reluctant to lose the feel of his body, even momentarily.

"Sure." He pulled back his head a little, not so much that their bodies separated, but enough so that he could look into her eyes. "Miss me a little?" he asked.

She nodded. "Of course."

His arms tightened, flattening her breasts against his hard chest, and he buried his face in her neck. "Miss me a lot?" he murmured, his tongue against her ear. "A whole lot?"

Her body quivered as his tongue traced the curve of her earlobe. "Yes," she whispered, glad that he couldn't see the blood rushing to her cheeks.

But he drew back just then and chuckled. "Why, Emily Asperson, I do believe you're blushing."

"I suppose I am." There wasn't much use in denying something so apparent. "But I'm not used to . . . this sort of thing. I've never brought anyone here. This is my private place."

His face grew serious. "I'm honored to be your first guest," he said soberly, and then he grinned. "Except for the Indians, of course."

He looked down at her jeans. "Whatever you think of Indians," he went on, his voice rich with amusement, "they knew how to dress their women. No stupid pants."

"We can fix that," she found herself saying and was conscious of a shock of surprise. She had never behaved like this before. Not with anyone.

"Right you are," he said. "But first the boots." He turned and crawled to her feet. With his back to her, he took one boot between his hands and yanked it off. The other soon followed.

As he returned to her side and reached for her belt buckle, she shook her head. "Nothing doing. *Your* boots come off next."

He grinned. "Don't worry, sweetheart. I'll take off my own boots."

She shook her head. "Foul! I cry foul. There's the old double standard again."

Moments later his boots and socks stood beside hers and her fingers moved to his belt. "Now we'll get rid of these."

His belt buckle yielded with surprising ease and soon he was wearing nothing but his shorts.

"My turn again," he said, pushing her down on the soft bank. She could feel each blade of grass against her bare back as he drew off her jeans and then her panties. Every cell in her body was sending clamoring reports of pleasure, of joy, to her brain. She smiled softly as Alex returned to her side, his shorts gone. The feel of the grass beneath her faded as his body met hers, as she moaned with pleasure at their meeting.

He covered her face with hot little kisses and buried his face in her neck. "The things you do to me," he groaned. "Are you sure you aren't a witch?"

She laughed softly, intoxicated with the feel of him. "This isn't New England. There are no witches out here. Only Indian medicine women."

He groaned again. "They're even worse." He kissed her ear. "Tell me, what kind of spell have you placed on me?"

It took her a moment to answer, for she found herself suddenly choked up, wishing with all her might that she *could* put a spell on him, *could* bind him to her.

"No spell," she said finally, hoping he would think the slight tremble in her voice was caused by passion. "Maybe it's spring fever."

He shook his head. "Nope. I've had that. This is different."

She held her breath, hoping he would say more, give her something concrete to build her dreams on. But he raised himself to his knees in their little hiding place and began to caress her. He knew her body so well, she thought. Better, perhaps, than she did herself.

She had often read that a man played on a woman's body as on a musical instrument, but she had never before realized how apt the metaphor was. It was as though she had no will of her own. Her bones and muscles seemed molten, ineffectual to move her. She was paralyzed under the fingers of the man who was bringing her so much pleasure. His hands caressed her trembling breasts, circled the rosy peaks that yearned for his touch, moved down to drift across the flat plane of her stomach to her white thighs, and then . . .

Everything melted together for her then, melted together and faded into one indistinct golden world that had its center deep, deep inside her. The pleasure was so intense that it almost approached pain and she could only moan incoherently and twist under his hands.

When she regained her senses, he was holding her in his arms and she realized that their loving had only just begun. "Oh, Alex," she panted.

His hands moved slowly across her back. "Take it easy, honey."

With one quick move he rolled them both over and was on top of her. "Yes, Alex. Oh, yes," she whispered against his hard shoulder as she opened herself eagerly to him.

For a moment she hung on the edge of ecstasy, but he lay still, allowing them both a moment's respite, so that when he began to move again she could feel the joy building inside her, layer upon layer, till it spread outward to encompass her whole panting, throbbing body in an aura of joy so intense that she cried out.

With his hoarse exclamation of fulfillment in her ears, she fell over the edge of eternity and drifted, blissful, in a cloud of contentment.

His weight was heavy upon her, but she welcomed it. As she regained her breath she thought with wry amusement that she needed to be held down or she might just float away.

His lips moved against her ear. "That was worth waiting for, sweetheart. Even better than I remembered."

And it was true. Their night together had been one of exploration and discovery. A wonderful night. But there had been something more to today. A feeling of . . . She searched her mind for the right word. A feeling of homecoming. Did he feel that, too? she wondered. But she dared not ask.

She might be fighting the double standard, but this early in a relationship it was foolish to ask too many questions about commitment. Better to wait, to give what was between them a chance to grow. As it had been growing. As it had grown this afternoon. She let herself relax again into the wonderful feel of his body on hers. Things were going along well, very well. And she was content with that. For now.

12

The next few days flew by. Mornings they practiced roping in the yard and she made herself treat him like any other student, this man who meant so much to her. Afternoons they rode out onto the prairie where they roped a few calves before they headed for her private spot.

In the ranch yard and at the table Emily managed to be only friendly with Alex. Her mother, she felt with an inner certainty, knew that they weren't spending all their afternoons roping, but she never said anything to indicate that knowledge. Her father was too busy enjoying Alex's company in the evenings to notice how his daughter was behaving. And her brothers were still going on down the road, the rodeo circuit keeping them far from home. For that, Emily was very grateful.

The last thing she needed was for one of them to stumble onto her secret. It was all right for them to get pink perfumed fan mail and whatever else the young girls who hung around the rodeo wanted to give them. But if they ever suspected what she and Alex were doing . . . Western men were very protective of their women. And in spite of her twenty-five years they thought of her as their baby sister and would be quick to avenge themselves on any man who had "taken advantage" of her.

The thought made her shiver. Once they were set off, Ted and Joe were practically impossible to stop. So it was a real blessing that they weren't around to foul things up. Alex would be leaving soon, she knew. And she didn't want to lose a precious moment with him.

As it was, she had five wonderful days before he turned to her and said, "I have to leave again tomorrow." They were lying in her secret spot, naked in each other's arms. A quick shiver spread over her at the thought of his leaving, but she managed not to say anything. He had his work to do. He had a living to make. And she had known. . . .

"I'm going to catch some more rodeos," he said. "Want to come with me?"

Her heart leapt into her throat at the thought of more lovely days and nights—with him. But she knew it couldn't be. "I . . . I'm sorry, Alex. I can't."

His eyes held disappointment, but not surprise. "Competing again?"

She nodded. "I . . . I hope you understand. I've got to do this."

His arm tightened around her. "Do *you* understand that I don't want to go to these rodeos, that I don't want to leave you?"

His words warmed her heart as the look in his eyes warmed her body. "Yes."

"Then why don't you think that I can understand

that you have to do your work? Your work is just as important to you as mine is to me."

She hugged him tightly. "Oh, Alex, you're the most wonderful man in the world."

His laughter boomed out. "And you're the most intelligent woman. For seeing that."

They laughed together then, but her heart was still heavy. She didn't want him to go. She didn't want to be separated from him. If it had only been a question of her own rodeoing, she would have been glad to give it up. But she had to keep in shape, had to compete all she could in preparation for that big event in Vegas. For the hundredth time she was tempted to tell him about it and for the hundredth time she stopped herself with the reminder that it was not her secret to tell.

She loved Alex and she trusted him. She would trust him with any part of her own life, but she could not betray the others. No matter what she thought of Alex, the rest of them didn't know him. And besides, she had given her solemn promise.

They lay quietly together for some minutes. She wanted to ask him how long he would be gone, when he was coming back. She didn't allow herself to think the word "if." But she remained silent, trying to convince herself that she wouldn't be lost without him and not getting very far at all.

He stirred, finally, his hand moving on her back. "I'll probably be gone a week or so. I've got to see some people down in Texas."

She nodded. A week was a very long time, she thought, and, realizing that she was missing him already, she snuggled closer against his side.

He raised his wrist and consulted his watch. "Do

you think we could be just a little late for dinner?" he asked, that glint in his eye.

She made herself chuckle. "I think so. Dad won't be home till late and Mom said she was going to make macaroni and cheese. It won't hurt that to set a bit."

"And your mother?"

His hand had already begun to move on her breast.

"What about my mother?"

"Will she . . ." He hesitated and Emily realized he was slightly embarrassed.

She laughed again, softly. "Don't worry about Mom. If she suspects, she won't say anything. She won't give us away."

His hand stopped moving and there was a strange note in his voice. "Give us away?" he repeated.

She wished she had kept her mouth shut. "My brothers are sort of old-fashioned," she began, then faltered to a halt.

"You mean they wouldn't like what I've been doing to their baby sister?"

"Something like that," she admitted.

His face was thoughtful. "Can't say that I blame them. I was always protective of my sisters, too. If I thought . . ."

"Hey," she said softly, her hand moving to caress him. "It's just you and me out here. And I like what you've been doing to me. I like it a lot."

His chuckle told her she had made her point. "You're right," he said, his voice husky. "And I like what you're doing to me."

He left the next morning. She went out to see him off. He didn't kiss her good-bye; they had done that the afternoon before. But she had a terrible desire to touch him once more before he left. And so just before he climbed in the old wagon she stuck out her hand. Surely no one would get suspicious from a mere handshake. "So long, Alex," she said, trying to keep her voice even.

His hand grasped hers, shook and squeezed it. "So long, Emily. I'll see you in about a week." His eyes held hers for a long moment and she felt the color staining her cheeks. There was not a bit of doubt in her mind. His eyes had spoken plainly of the homecoming that he was already envisioning.

He released her hand. "Till then," he said softly.

"Till then," she repeated. And added, "Drive carefully now."

"I will."

She stood watching till the car was out of sight, the dust that marked its passage hidden in the swell of the prairie. Then she turned to the stable and saddled Gypsy. She needed a ride, needed it badly. She had to get her head together, stop mooning around about Alex. There was a job to be done. And a lot of people were depending on her to do it.

She had just led Gypsy through the corral gate and swung into the saddle when she saw a cloud of dust coming up the lane to the house. Her heart began to pound in her throat. Had Alex forgotten something? Had he changed his mind about going? She stared at the cloud as it grew closer.

Then she saw it, the brown pickup that was generating all that dust, and her heart fell into her boots. It was Jerry.

Now, of all times, she didn't want to see Jerry. She considered swinging Gypsy's head toward the prairie and galloping off, but she restrained herself. That was a cowardly thing to do. And useless besides. Jerry was perfectly capable of sitting there and waiting till she got back. Or, more probably, saddling one of the horses in the corral and coming after her. She wouldn't dare go to her special place when he might find her there. No, it was better to stay here and get it over with, disagreeable as it might be. With a sigh she swung down and waited.

He slowed as he neared the ranch and she watched silently as he opened the door and climbed out. His right wrist was in a cast, she noted, and noted, too, that there was no rush of terror in her heart, no fear such as she would have felt had she seen Alex wearing something like that.

"Hi, Em."

"Hi, Jerry." She knew he was waiting for her to ask, so she did. "What happened?"

He grinned sheepishly. "Dumb bull tossed me off and I fell on it. Gonna be out of action for a few weeks."

Emily nodded. When he said a few weeks, that was all he meant. The minute the cast was off Jerry would be back on a bull. Now if he'd fallen on his left wrist, he'd probably still be competing, since he didn't need to hold on with it, only to keep it in the air. She sighed. Rodeo men were like that. They didn't let injuries stop them.

"I thought . . ." He hesitated. "I'm sorry about flying off the handle like I did," he finally went on. "But when you couldn't go to the dance with me, I was real disappointed."

She nodded, astonishment keeping her silent. Jerry had never apologized to her for anything before. This was certainly a new approach.

"I thought . . ." Again he hesitated. "That is, if you'll forgive me, how about having dinner with me? Say tomorrow night? Or the next? Whenever you're free."

She was still amazed at this new Jerry, so she was slow to answer. But he waited patiently. Her thoughts were tumbling. She didn't really want to have dinner with Jerry. She wanted to be with Alex. Only Alex. But it was hardly fair to blame Jerry for that. This was a genuine peace overture he was making to her. And knowing his pride, she knew, too, that it had cost him something to make it. "Tomorrow night sounds good," she said. "We'll just forget about the other day."

"Good." His face brightened. "Pick you up about seven?"

She nodded. "Okay."

"Okay. See you then."

She caught the relief on his face as he turned away and she felt she could almost read his thoughts. He was glad to have the difficult apology over—she had no doubt it was difficult for him—and he had decided not to push his luck.

"See you then," she called after him and turned to the patiently waiting mare.

The next evening while she was waiting for Jerry, the phone rang. She jumped up from where she'd been sitting in the kitchen talking to her mother. "I'll get it."

In the den she sank down into the big leather chair that stood behind her father's desk. "Double A Ranch," she said. "Emily Asperson speaking."

"I want to talk to Alex Calloway. Put him on."

The voice was harsh and domineering and Emily felt her back stiffen, but her inbred courtesy prevailed. "Mr. Calloway isn't here. May I take a message?"

"Of course you may. Confound that man! Why can't I ever reach him?"

Emily made no reply to this obviously rhetorical question, but she knew her heart had begun to pound and the hand that held the phone had gone suddenly clammy.

"Well, never mind that. Just tell him this. Are you ready to write this down?"

Emily bit her lip. She would not say "yes, ma'am" to this . . . this . . . "I'm ready," she said, managing to keep her tone even.

"Good. Tell him Mrs. Livingstone called."

Emily's hand wavered, then continued writing. Mrs. Harvey Wallace Livingstone III *was* like a talking bulldozer.

"Tell him to hurry up. I liked the outline he gave me and I'm anxious to see the first chapter."

Emily forgot her anger as fear swamped her. "You're anxious to see the first chapter of the book," she repeated.

There was such hesitancy in her voice that the redoubtable Mrs. Livingstone boomed, "That's right. The book about the rodeo. Awful sport. Absolutely impossible. Criminal. Inhumane." She paused and took a deep breath. "Sorry. Forgot myself there for a minute. You tell that boy to call me. We contracted for a book and I don't aim to wait forever." And without so much as a good-bye Mrs. Livingstone hung up.

For several seconds Emily sat motionless, the receiver still to her ear. Alex! Doing a book for that woman! An attack on the rodeo! It seemed unbelievable. But he had used her. They came back to her now—all his questions about the animals and their injuries. She had thought him such a sensitive man. And all the time he had just been doing his research! She had trusted him and he had betrayed her.

The noise the telephone was making finally penetrated and she hung it up and pressed her trembling hands to her temples. How could he? How could he do this to her? She swallowed over the lump in her throat. She couldn't cry now. Jerry would be coming.

The sound of a motor outside made her straighten her shoulders. There he was. She would have to think about this later. She got to her feet and went to the door, fixing a smile of welcome on her face.

"Hello, Jerry." Evidently he saw nothing wrong with her smile, for he gave her one in return.

"You look great," he said.

She nodded absently and took the arm he offered her. It was as if she had become two separate people, she thought, as he helped her into his pickup. One of them was chatting and smiling at Jerry, having herself a grand old time, and the other was sobbing and screaming. Why, why had Alex done this terrible thing to her? Why had he betrayed her trust?

The whole evening went on in the same way. She ate her dinner, she talked about this and that, she danced with Jerry, noting that his arms didn't feel at all like Alex's and then reminding herself that that was good, that Alex's arms had held false comfort, fake security.

She moved a little closer to Jerry. He had his faults, but he would never have hurt her as Alex had. Steeped in her pain, she ignored the one sane segment of her mind that chose that moment to remind her that Jerry *couldn't* hurt her like Alex had for the simple reason that he didn't mean as much to her.

Emboldened by her closeness, Jerry suggested that they start home. The watching Emily saw the look in his eyes, but the one who was doing all the pretending appeared not to notice it and the kind of trouble it was clearly foreshadowing.

When Jerry pulled into the ranch yard, the house was dark. "Everyone's gone to bed," he said, his voice holding satisfaction.

"Yes, we all get up early."

"Let's take a little walk."

"Okay."

The watching Emily wanted to take that other one aside and shake her. Didn't she know, couldn't she see, what was on Jerry's mind?

He opened the truck door and helped her down, pulling her arm through his as they turned toward the stable. "Pretty moon tonight," he said.

"Yes. Very pretty."

As soon as they were out of sight of the house, shielded from prying eyes by the shadow of the stable, he pulled her into his arms and kissed her passionately. She tried to respond, she wanted to respond. She wanted it desperately. The thought screamed through her mind: Let him kiss you. Jerry can help you forget. Forget Alex.

She yielded her mouth to his, her body to the pressure of his arms. She tried to feel something—passion, desire, even affection. But she felt nothing. She might as well have been kissing a tree. There was no current, no connection—nothing to pass between them. Recognizing this, and the futility of what she was doing, she tried to free herself. But Jerry misunderstood her struggles. "That's better, baby. Old Jerry'll take care of you."

Her reaction to his words was as startling to Emily as it was to him. The separated parts of herself rushed together with a great surge of outrage and she wrenched herself free and glared at him.

Jerry stared at her in surprise. "Hey, what's the matter?"

Her anger faded just a little. She had more or less asked for this clinch. So she didn't sound as nasty as she felt when she said, "I'm not your baby. And I don't need to be taken care of." Repeating his words made her anger start building again. She turned back toward the house. "Good night, Jerry. I don't think we'd better see each other anymore."

She meant to leave it at that, but he grabbed her wrist and jerked her to a stop. "What the hell are you talking about? You've been making up to me all evening. And now you tell me we're not going to see each other anymore? Well, I'm not some dumb steer to be shoved around. I want some answers. I want to know what the hell is going on!"

She pried futilely at his grip on her wrist. "It's very simple," she said. "I thought we could be friends. But now I've changed my mind." She was tired, so tired. "I just want to go in and go to bed." The words were hardly out of her mouth before she realized her mistake. This was not the time to mention bed.

His reaction confirmed that. "Yeah! Sure!" In all the times she had seen Jerry angry, and they were not a few, she had never seen him this enraged. "What'sa matter? Your little playmate split? I bet you haven't been going to bed alone, have you?"

She considered screaming for help, then thought

better of it. There was no sense in making a big scene. "I don't think that's any of your business," she said as coldly as she could. "You're not my keeper."

"No, and I'm damn glad. Any woman that'd sleep with that dumb little easterner ain't no concern of mine."

Words of defense rushed to her lips, hot angry words. Alex wasn't a big man, but he wasn't little, either. And he certainly wasn't dumb. The pain came then—sharp and quick—as she remembered the way he'd fooled her.

She took a deep breath. "I have work to do tomorrow, Jerry." She looked pointedly at the hand still clamped around her wrist. She knew a certain karate trick that would land him flat in the dust. But she wouldn't do that unless she had to. She really was partly responsible for the events of the evening. She realized that she had sort of led him on.

She raised her eyes to his. "I'm sorry, Jerry. I really am. I shouldn't have gone out with you tonight. But I felt I owed you something after that nice apology. As far as the rest of it goes . . ." She shrugged. "We're not right for each other. We never really were. If you think about it a little, you'll see that."

She saw the confirmation in his eyes and hurried on. "You probably know it already. For the sake of Joe and Ted, if not for our own, let's part friends."

He considered this for a few minutes, then he dropped her wrist. "Maybe you're right," he said. "Maybe we're not so good for each other. I don't know about that. But I do know that I don't want to lose your brothers' friendship."

"You won't," she said. "You can be sure of that."

"Good." He hesitated, then turned toward his

truck. He was almost there when he swung around to face her. "I can't help it," he said. "I've gotta say it. I think you're making a big mistake. That guy's not your type. You're gonna be sorry."

She watched him drive off and only then did she speak aloud the words that had sprung to her lips. "I already am, Jerry. I already am."

13

·-∞∞∞∞∞∞∞∞-·

The days passed—bright, sunny, Montana days—but there was no sunshine for Emily. She worked herself hard, really hard, practicing every day, helping her mother in the kitchen, even scrubbing down the bunkhouse. Anything to keep busy, to so exhaust herself that she could fall into bed at night and have no trouble sleeping.

Several times she noticed her mother looking at her curiously. Once Noreen Asperson even opened her mouth to say something, then snapped it shut again. Emily was grateful for her mother's silence. She didn't think she could talk about it yet. Maybe after Alex came back, maybe after she had had it out with him. Maybe.

She couldn't think of anything he could say to her, any reason whatsoever for this horrible thing he had done to her. But she intended to hear him out. She needed that. She needed a confrontation with the man who had hurt her so badly. Once they'd had it out, once she'd told him all the things she'd been rehearsing, then she could conclude that part of her life and begin again.

She would have to begin again—at least where men were concerned. But she knew she'd been right about Jerry. Even if Alex had never come into her life, she and Jerry would have parted eventually. He represented all the things she most disliked in men. He was arrogant and conceited and a complete male chauvinist. Just like her brothers. Not fit company for a woman who thought of herself as an adult.

And Alex? Alex had seemed different. Sensitive, understanding, seeing her as a human being, not some kind of thing to be used or a child to be humored. Oh, yes, she thought bitterly, Alex had *seemed* different. But he had turned out to be just like the rest. Worse, even. For he had seemed worthy of the trust she had given him, the love. And he had tricked her. Rage and humiliation warred within her. One moment she wanted to scream and throw things at him, the next she wanted to run away and hide because she had let herself become so vulnerable.

Thoughts like these plagued her constantly, even when she went up to Wolf Point in the middle of the week to compete. Luckily, Cherry was not there and Emily didn't know most of the others. She'd been tempted to stay home. The way she felt she wasn't sure she could even go through with the plan. She wasn't going to be any good in Vegas if she didn't get herself straightened out. But she would; she had to, because they were depending on her.

Since Cherry wasn't there, Emily didn't compete in the team roping. And it was a good thing, she thought as she backed Gypsy against the rail and settled the piggin' string between her teeth. She didn't want to be responsible for Cherry's losing any more day money. Her thoughts moved to that other time—when the calf had turned and evaded the loop, that time when Alex had comforted her afterward.

She dropped her head in the nod that signaled the release of the calf. No time to think of Alex now. Time only to think of the familiar ritual. Gypsy's legs bunched beneath her as the little mare bounded after the calf. This one was a runner, away like an arrow.

Time took on an unusual distortion. The calf seemed to run for hours, the rope that swung heavily in her hand seemed to have been there forever. And when it finally sailed through the air, it was like watching a slow-motion movie. The loop came closer and closer to the calf's head. Yet so certain was she that something would go wrong, that she would miss, that when it finally settled around the calf's neck only habit propelled her off the mare and down the rope to make the tie.

As she raised her hands, it seemed that hours had passed since Gypsy had first burst from the chute. Even before the announcer gave her time, she knew it hadn't been good enough to win. This thing with Alex was affecting everything she did.

She tried to think of something else, anything else, as she fed and watered and rubbed Gypsy down after the second go-round. But she couldn't keep Alex and their coming confrontation out of her mind. She leaned her head against the mare's warm neck. "Oh, Gypsy," she whispered. "I wish he'd come. I want to get this over with."

The mare turned and whuffled against Emily's neck in sympathy, her clear brown eyes full of love. Patting the glossy neck, Emily raised her head. "You're a wonderful friend, Gypsy. The best friend a girl could have."

She left the mare, finally, heading toward the motel. She could have driven home that evening, but her mother had elicited a promise that she would wait till morning to start. She was glad now that she had given it. She was dead tired. Unfortunately, the exhaustion she felt was more mental than physical. She wouldn't dare go to bed early, and she'd have to go out and take a long walk before bedtime. But right now she was going to take a shower.

The motel room felt comfortably cool after the sun's heat and she closed the door behind her, wondering if she'd forgotten to turn off the air conditioner before she left. She started across the room to check and halted in midstride as a figure half raised itself from the bed. "Hi. How'd you do today?"

For a moment she was paralyzed. Now that he was here, now that she could have her confrontation, she wanted to forget the whole thing, to run into his arms for comfort. What a stupid reaction, she told herself. She straightened her shoulders. "Hello, Alex. How did you get in here?"

He sat up. "I told the clerk I was your brother. She believed me."

"I see." She hadn't known her voice could sound so weary. "With the help of a little cash, I suppose."

He grinned. "Actually, that wasn't necessary." His grin faded as he scanned her face. "You didn't win, huh? Did the loop miss?"

"No. I didn't miss. But I didn't win. My time wasn't good enough."

He got up from the bed and came toward her. "I'm sorry, honey."

She almost let him reach her, almost let him take

her in his arms. But at the last moment sanity asserted itself. "No! Don't touch me."

He stared at her in bewilderment. "It's not losing today. It's something else. Emily, what on earth is wrong?" His eyes searched her face. "Honey, have you been sick?"

She laughed at that. Even she herself recognized the hysterical quality of that laugh. "I guess you could say that. Yes, I've been sick."

He took another step toward her and she backed away. "No, don't."

"Okay, okay. You look beat. Let's sit down. Tell me what it is."

Her legs seemed to have turned to water and she sank down gratefully into a chair. He settled on the edge of the bed, his face anxious. "Please, honey, tell me what this is all about."

She took a deep breath. The endearment hurt, seeing him hurt, wanting him hurt. But she had to go through with this.

"It's about a phone call," she said.

His expression showed only bewilderment.

"From Mrs. Harvey Wallace Livingstone the third."

His eyes clouded over, closing her out. "What did she want?" he asked.

"She wanted the first chapter of her book," she said. "She liked the outline. She wants to see the book." She took a long, shuddering breath. "Your exposé of the rodeo. Of its brutal, cruel, inhumane treatment of animals." Her calmness left her, suddenly and swiftly, and she began to tremble. "Oh, Alex, how could you? How could you do a book for that horrible old woman? How could you attack the rodeo? How could you lie to me?" She broke down then, sobbing into her hands.

He was silent for a few moments, waiting till her sobs subsided somewhat. "I didn't lie to you."

Astonishment made her raise her head and stare at him.

"Think a minute," he went on. "I didn't lie. I just didn't tell you everything."

"It's the same thing. And you pumped me—about the treatment of the animals." Even through her tears she could see the pain in his face, but she hardened her heart.

"Of course I did," he replied. "If you set out to expose something, you can hardly walk up to people and say, 'Look, I'm writing an exposé on your favorite activity. Give me all the dirt.'"

"But I'm not just anyone!" All the pain of her betrayal was in that sentence and he flinched.

"Of course you're not. But in the beginning—when we were strangers—I didn't know what was going to happen between us."

"But later . . ."

"Later I was afraid." His eyes darkened. "When you asked about the letter, I put you off. I was afraid you'd be upset with me."

"But . . . but you knew I'd find out eventually."

He shook his head. "No, I didn't. Because I decided not to do the book. I couldn't do the book she wanted. I couldn't find evidence to warrant it. It looks to me like the cowboys are the ones that need protection, not the animals. I told her that when I returned her expense money. Right after I left here last time."

He saw her disbelief. "I'll show you the canceled check when it comes back." His eyes searched her face. "I know I should have told you. But what we have is so special. And I knew how you felt about the rodeo. I thought you'd never need to know." His eyes held hers, full of pleading, full of . . . "Please, Emily, will you forgive me?"

Her thoughts were a chaotic jumble. She wanted to believe him, to admit that he was not the monster she'd been imagining him all week. But she was afraid. The switch was too sudden. There had to be a hitch somewhere. "I . . . I don't know."

He rose from the bed and came to kneel at her feet. "Please, Emily, don't let this spoil what we have. I admit I made a mistake. I'm sorry. I won't keep things from you again. I promise."

There was no way she could refuse the plea in those eyes. With a sigh she let go of all the bad thoughts and feelings she'd been piling up as a wall between them. There was no longer any need for them. This was Alex kneeling here, the man she loved, the man she trusted. And he was worthy of her trust. She moistened her lips. "Yes, Alex. I forgive you." To her surprise a giggle came bubbling to her lips. "I just hope Mrs. Livingstone doesn't call again. She *does* sound like a bulldozer."

His face lit up as he got to his feet and pulled her into his arms. "Hello, darling. I've missed you awfully."

Her sigh came from the bottom of her heart and she whispered against his neck, "Oh, Alex, I missed you, too."

"Now that that's settled," he said, "let's have a hello kiss."

As she felt the warmth of his arms around her, as she raised her face to his, she felt a sense of well-being spread over her. If only things could stay like this. Vegas would be a piece of cake if only she were sure of

Alex's love. His lips came down on hers then, driving rational thought away, and she clung to him, savoring the feel of his hard body against her own.

When he released her mouth, she was trembling and weak. But from desire, not fear. He pulled her down on the bed and knelt to pull off her boots. Then he was there beside her, his arm around her. "Do you have any plans for the evening?" he asked, kissing the tip of her nose.

She shook her head.

He smiled in relief. "That's good. What about tomorrow? Meeting someone for breakfast or lunch?"

"No. Cherry's not here. And I . . ." She decided to let that pass. It seemed incredible that less than an hour ago she'd been so upset that she hadn't wanted to see or talk to anyone.

"Then I have you all to myself."

"I have to get home tomorrow. Mom will worry if I don't."

He kissed the point of her chin. "Call her in the morning and tell her you're leaving later. If you want to, of course."

She almost laughed out loud at that. There was nothing in the world that she wanted more than to be with this man. She reached up a finger to trace the curve of his lips. "I want to," she said.

She looked at him curiously. "Hey, how'd you know where to find me? I didn't tell you I was coming here."

His smile was mischievous and the fingers of his free hand moved to the buttons on her shirt. "Your mother told me. She also told me, or rather suggested—" his eyes sparkled—"that I come up and watch you."

"It's a long drive," Emily said. "A very long drive."

"I know." He kissed her earlobe, his tongue making

little circles against it while his hand stole inside her shirt and curled around her breast. "But when I thought of you here—in a room—by yourself . . ." He chuckled. "At least, I hoped you'd be by yourself. And your mother was sure you'd be staying all night . . ."

"She made me promise I would."

He laughed as he slid her shirt from her shoulders, as his fingers found the hook to her bra. "I like your mother." He paused. "Do you think she knows about . . . us? What we've been doing?"

She sighed under his moving fingers and nuzzled his neck. "She hasn't said so. But I'm pretty sure she's guessed."

"That must mean she likes me, then. Since she told me where to come. Where you'd be."

"I suppose so."

"And your father? Will she tell him?"

She nibbled at his ear. "I don't think so. I don't think he knows. He might not like it." She faltered. "Not because it's you, but because . . ."

"I know. Because no one is good enough for you."

She sighed again. "I wish I knew how you got to be so smart."

He pushed himself to his knees and reached for her belt buckle. "I was sort of a father to my sisters," he said. "I experienced a lot of fatherly feelings." He pulled her jeans down over her hips, then her panties. He drew in his breath. "You're even more beautiful than I remembered."

A slow blush spread over her body as his eyes devoured her and she longed to feel him against her. She raised her arms to him. "Hurry, please," she whispered, startled that she should say such a thing.

But she saw that it pleased him. His smile widened as he shed his own clothes in record time.

As his body met hers she sighed in contentment. "Oh, that's good," she murmured against his shoulder. "I missed the feel of you."

He hugged her tightly. "I missed you so much I couldn't sleep at night. I kept waking up wanting you. And I had this funny, nagging feeling, as if something were wrong and I should get back to you right—" He paused. "I'll be darned! The feeling was right. There was something wrong. How about that?"

She didn't answer. She knew that sometimes people had feelings like that, ways of knowing how other people were. Maybe the connection between herself and Alex was so strong that her distress had somehow reached him. It was a comforting thought and she held it close, not daring to examine its implications any further.

"Oh," he said, laughter in his voice. "Here we are all undressed and I forgot to ask if you've had your dinner."

"I know you, Alex Calloway," she teased. "I bet you didn't forget at all. You're just a sex fiend."

He assumed an injured expression. "Well, we could always get dressed again. *If* you're absolutely starving and too weak from hunger to do anything else."

The laughter bubbled from her. It was so good to be able to laugh again. "No, I'm not too weak from hunger. Besides, I'm a sex fiend, too." And she turned to him hungrily. "We can eat later. If we want to."

The rich, warm sound of his laughter delighted her almost as much as the feel of his body against hers. Then his hands and his mouth were busy upon her and she lost all sense of time and place until she came floating hazily back from bliss and fell asleep against his shoulder.

14

A week later Emily stood before a mirror in a Las Vegas motel room. Wearing bulky clothing and her hat pulled low, she hoped she could pass for a man. She was small, of course, and slender. But so were many rodeo cowboys. With no makeup and no feminine curves, she should be able to get through it.

She sighed and turned away from the mirror. If only she'd been able to tell Alex about the plan. Things had been so good between them that night in Wolf Point. And before they'd parted the next day he'd asked her to meet him in Vegas. His request had taken her by surprise and she'd had to think fast. She wasn't absolutely sure he'd believe her story about not going, about having to compete elsewhere. And if he asked where . . . She'd held her breath, but he'd only shaken his head and said he'd see her afterward at the ranch.

Now she was stuck in this motel room, afraid to go out except to take care of Gypsy. For if Alex saw her it could blow the whole thing.

Liz McGuire, the reporter who was related to Marilyn, was here. She had eaten with Cherry and the others last night while Emily had hidden out in the room, waiting for the meal they'd brought back with them. Liz had her story all written. Everything was going the way it should. The rest was up to E. M. Asperson.

Emily had never been a cursing person, but living all those years in the vicinity of her brothers had made more than a few choice phrases available to her. She muttered one of them now. Why had she consented to this crazy plan, anyway? The men who ran the rodeo weren't going to change it. Things would go right on in the same old unfair way. Whatever happened here in Vegas, even if she won, would soon be forgotten.

She threw herself down on the bed. Why not face the truth? she asked herself. She was afraid, scared to death, that she would fail her friends, would let them down, and all their plans would be for nothing.

That was why she kept telling herself that what they were doing wouldn't change anything. Because she was so scared of failing them she had to make the whole thing seem unimportant.

But whatever the men might think, and however soon what happened was forgotten, it was vitally important to her friends. They had put their time, their money, their faith in her. She couldn't fail them. She just couldn't.

A glance at her watch made her catch her breath. It was time to go to the arena, a trip she would make alone since she was less conspicuous that way, and less likely to be recognized by someone who knew all of them.

The trip was uneventful and she soon had Gypsy saddled and ready. Much sooner than she felt ready for it, she was putting the piggin' string between her teeth and backing Gypsy into the corner. "Please don't let me fail them," she prayed as she gave the nod that released the calf.

Again there was the terrible sense of slow motion. Gypsy bounded forward, the loop sailed out from Emily's hand as the familiar litany repeated itself in her head. Swing. Throw. Jerk. Pitch.

Her foot was already out of the stirrup as the loop settled over the calf's head, yet the run down the rope seemed to take forever. She grabbed the calf and brought it down. The loop went easily over a front foot, almost wrapped itself into a half hitch. She raised her hands. The calf struggled briefly but could not free itself.

As she remounted Gypsy the announcer's voice rolled out over the crowd. "E. M. Asperson did that tidy bit of roping and tying in nine point two seconds. Darn good time for a beginner."

And it was, she thought, as she took care of Gypsy and made her way back to the room. Darn good time for anyone, but it was just a beginning.

She didn't hang around waiting to hear how the others were doing because she didn't dare. The more time she spent where there were people, the greater her chances of being discovered. And there was Alex to worry about, too. He might be behind the chutes, researching. She couldn't afford to let him see her.

The motel room was empty when she reached it

and she took off her boots and stretched out, trying to relax. There were still more go-rounds. She had a good start, but that was all.

She was just dozing off when the door opened and Cherry and Marilyn came barreling in. "You were great, Em. Just great."

"Wonderful," Marilyn agreed. "We're going to do it. I know we're going to do it."

Emily shook her head. "I'm not so sure. You know how many things can go wrong."

Cherry shrugged. "No sense in thinking about that. It doesn't help."

Emily sighed. "No, I suppose not."

"We're going to get something to eat," Cherry went on. "What—"

A sharp rap on the door brought Emily to her feet. She slipped into the bathroom as Cherry went to open it. "Why, hello, Mr. Calloway."

"Hello, Cherry. I want to see Emily."

"Emily? Emily's not with us."

"She's not with you?"

From her hiding place in the bathroom, she heard the surprise in his voice. "Where is she, then?"

"Home, I guess. Anyway, she's not here."

Emily's heart sank. Why hadn't she thought to warn her friends, to give them the right story to tell? But she hadn't expected Alex to come knocking on the door like this. There were lots and lots of motels in Vegas.

"Well . . ." He still didn't sound convinced. "If you see her, tell her I'm looking for her."

"I will, Mr. Calloway. As soon as we get home."

The door closed, there were a few moments of silence, then Cherry called softly, "You can come out now."

Slowly Emily left the sanctuary of the bathroom. "Do you think he believed you?" she asked.

Cherry shrugged. "I guess so. It doesn't matter. I passed him in the lobby. Probably he thought we came down together."

"Probably," Emily repeated, but she knew there was more to it than that. Alex's voice had held anxiety. Well, she couldn't think about that now. She couldn't see him till the rodeo was over. There was just too much at stake.

"We'll go get dinner now," Cherry said, breaking into her thoughts. "What'll we bring you?"

"It doesn't matter. I'm not hungry."

"I'll bring you a good dinner," Cherry said firmly. "You have to eat."

Emily nodded. She was too exhausted to argue over a stupid thing like food. She was almost too tired to eat, she thought, as the door closed behind her friends and she threw herself back down on the bed. But Cherry was right. When they brought the food back, she would force herself to eat it.

She set to work to relax, to get the tensions out of her body. Using the techniques she had learned in school, she began counting silently backward from ten, envisioning herself going down, deeper and deeper, into her unconscious with each number.

She had reached four and was beginning to feel detached from the world around her when there was a hurried knock on the door. What had Cherry forgotten now? she wondered, pushing herself to her feet and reaching for the door. Probably her keys.

But it was not Cherry who stood in the corridor. It was Alex Calloway. She drew back, trying to shut the door. But he was too quick for her. He pushed past her and closed the door behind him. "So you *are* here."

There wasn't much point in denying that, so she remained silent, waiting.

He swung around to face her. "What the hell is going on?" he asked.

"I . . . I just got in." Would he believe that? "They canceled my rodeo so I decided to come down here and join the others."

He shook his head angrily. "It won't work, Emily. When you're 'not here,' you shouldn't leave your boots in plain sight of the door. I'd know those boots anywhere."

She felt the color flooding her cheeks. "I . . . I didn't want to lie to you, Alex. But . . . but we don't want anyone to know I'm here."

Her apology did nothing to soothe his feelings and he remained standing, glaring at her. "Why not?" he demanded, taking a step closer.

Overwhelmed by a desire to step into his arms, she struggled to control herself. "I can't tell you," she whispered, knowing that this would not satisfy him, knowing that nothing less than the truth would do that. Knowing, too, that the truth was not hers to give him.

"Oh, you can't tell me." Every word was an accusation. He grabbed her upper arms in a grip that made her wince. "Shall I tell *you*, then, E. M. Asperson?"

She was silent. She couldn't tell him, but if he had guessed . . .

"That was *you* I saw out there. E. M. Asperson, with his nine point two time, who won today's round."

"I won?" she cried, not immediately realizing that she had given herself away in that moment of delight.

She could not help the momentary surge of relief that went through her. Even if she didn't win the whole thing they could probably do the article now.

"You did," he growled. "I could hardly believe my eyes when I saw you coming out of that chute. I almost had a heart attack."

Something about that rankled her. "I don't see why. I'm perfectly capable of handling myself. I won, didn't I?"

He shook her in exasperation. "Yeah, you won. But those calves are a hundred pounds heavier than what you're used to. That arena's no place for you. You'll get hurt."

She jerked herself free of his hold and faced him defiantly. "Oh, now I see. What you mean is the arena's no place for any woman. We're too weak and fragile to be doing important things like men do."

"Damn it, I didn't say that," he cried, jamming his hands into his pockets in exasperation.

"No, but you *thought* it. Well, just you listen to me. I'm a grown woman. An adult. I'm not an idiot! Not a child! And you're not my keeper." Her breasts were heaving now and her eyes blazed. "So just leave me alone!"

"And let you get yourself killed? Nothing doing. What the hell's going on, anyway? How'd you manage to get into the competition? And why?"

"I can't tell you that."

"You damn well better," he threatened. "Because I'm not leaving here till you do." And he plopped down on the protesting bed.

She heard the determination in his voice. Could she trust him? she wondered. But she almost had to. He had guessed so much. And he could ruin everything if he went to the officials now. It looked like she would have to tell him. Aware that her knees were trembling, she lowered herself into a chair and began.

"There's a bunch of us. Cherry and some others. We all feel the same way—about the unfairness." She glanced at him. He nodded, but his face didn't soften.

"Well, we got together the permit money and we sent it in—for E. M. Asperson. And if—when—I win, we'll announce that I'm a woman. Then the world will see that women are as good as men."

He was silent for so long that she couldn't stand it. "I wanted to tell you, but I couldn't. It wasn't my secret to tell."

Finally he spoke, but his voice hadn't softened. "So you put me off with that story about competing somewhere else."

"Yes."

His eyes were cloudy as he got to his feet. "Stop now, Emily. You've made your point. You won today's round. Give your story to the papers and stop."

"I can't." The words came out without conscious thought, but they were the right words. "They're depending on me."

"And what about me?" he said. "Don't I count?"

"Of course you count." She was having trouble talking, the lump in her throat was growing. "But this hasn't anything to do with you. I made a promise and I have to keep it."

"It was a foolish promise," he said. "It's that damn loyalty thing, isn't it? Your friends mean more to you than I do. You didn't trust me enough to tell me the truth and now you don't care enough about me to stop this foolishness."

The tears had reached her eyes now and moisture made it hard to see him. For a second she was tempted to throw herself into his arms and agree to anything he wanted. But it was only for a second. However wrong he thought she was, however foolish he thought her promise, it *was* a promise. And she would stick by it.

She took refuge in the only emotion she could safely reveal—anger. "You're being very unfair, you know. You talk about trust. Did you trust *me?* No, you didn't. I never asked you to break your word, to desert your friends. I never asked you for anything."

With dismay she realized that that was not entirely true and she hurried on. "You stand there and tell me that if I cared for you, I wouldn't be doing this. Well, I can say the same thing! I can say that if *you* cared for *me,* you wouldn't be doing this to me! If you cared for me, you'd be cheering me on!"

She stopped, unable to hold back the tears.

He gave her one hard glance and turned toward the door, his white face set in angry lines. "I guess that settles it. We're both agreed. We don't care about each other." He paused at the door, his hand on the knob. "You're too damn stubborn to listen to reason, but that doesn't mean I have to stay around and watch you make a fool of yourself. Or worse yet, get yourself maimed or killed." And the door closed behind him with a solid thump.

For one grief-stricken minute she stood, frozen in place, then she threw herself onto the bed and let the tears come. She did love him, she loved him a great deal. But that didn't mean she was willing to become a different person for him, to turn her back on her friends and break her promise. How could love ask that of her? Love was supposed to make a person better, not worse.

Time, and the rodeo, went on. When her friends returned that night, she didn't mention Alex's second visit. She simply ate what they brought her and went to bed. And the next day, and the next, and the next, she competed, giving it everything she had.

There was no word from Alex. No sight of him, though sometimes she couldn't keep from searching the crowd for his face.

The night before the final go-round, the girls all gathered in the room. Emily had begun to hate the sight of it, this room that had become almost a prison to her. She was quiet and withdrawn. All her concentration was focused on winning. Until that was done she would resolutely keep from thinking about Alex. First she would do what must be done—for the sake of her friends and her own conscience. Only when that was over would she be free to think about her personal problems.

Her friends were all in high spirits. Her times had been so good that now she ranked second in her event. Just that day she'd had to do some quick stepping to avoid a TV reporter, intent on doing an interview with this "rising star."

But all the excitement around her did not really reach her. It was early yet to celebrate. It was true that even if she lost tomorrow, she had done well enough to make their point. But although they weren't saying so, she knew that her friends would not really be happy unless she won. So many years of being put down had made each of them angry. And they saw this as their chance to get even. She'd been wrong in thinking that the outcome of this rodeo would soon be forgotten. As long as any of these young women lived, what happened here would be vitally important. She could imagine them telling their daughters and grand-daughters. And the whole thing rested on her. Surrounded by her laughing friends she had never felt more alone.

15

The next afternoon, her teeth clenched on the piggin' string, her loop ready in her hand, Emily backed Gypsy into the corner of the chute. The prayer she'd been saying all week went silently through her mind again. If she could just do it right this last time.

Then she nodded and the calf was freed. It was no different from any other go-round, the same thing happened to time, stretching it out forever. The loop hung for what seemed like minutes over the calf's head before it finally settled into place. Her run down the rope was nightmarishly long; she thought it would never end. Even the piggin' string loop seemed to hesitate before it dropped over the calf's front hoof. By the time she had made the tie and raised her hands, she had lost all sense of time, had no idea how well she'd done.

"And that's it, ladies and gents. This newcomer,

E. M. Asperson, has beaten all the old pros. Just look at this time. Eight point five seconds. Terrific!"

Emily tried to feel some elation as she moved toward the press box where Liz McGuire was waiting. Maybe that TV reporter who'd been after her would be there, too. If so, she was going to get a lot more than an interview with a "rising star." A whole lot more.

The press box was full of chattering reporters. "Mr. Asperson," said the young woman who'd been after her before, almost pouncing on her as she came in the door. "You're quite a mystery man."

Emily took off her hat. She was surrounded by a ring of expectant faces. A great wave of fatigue hit her suddenly and she wondered what the reporters would do if their "rising star" suddenly keeled over. She could see Liz's eager face in the background, and several other women reporters whose faces made her wonder if they already knew her secret. She took a deep breath.

"I'm not a mystery man," she said. "I'm not a *man* at all." The noise around her ended abruptly. "My name is Emily Asperson." The words sounded loud in the silent little room. "I'm a woman. I compete on the women's circuit."

Stunned silence was the only response to this for some moments. Then she saw one of the officials eyeing her with shock. "Damn it," he muttered. "She's right. That's Joe Asperson's girl."

Emily waited for the deluge of questions, but the silence continued. "You realize that you're disqualified," another official said finally. "This is a men's rodeo."

"And women aren't allowed," Emily added. "Yes. I

realize that. That's why I'm here. Women *should* be allowed to compete with men. We have the ability. We can win. That's the point of my being here today," she continued. "To prove that women can compete with men and even win."

Her statement broke the spell of silence and questions came at her from all directions. It was almost an hour later before she could break away, and when she reached the motel room it was empty. A big note on the mirror proclaimed "Gone to the steak house to celebrate. Meet us there."

Wearily, she stripped off her clothes and climbed into the shower. The hot water eased away some of the tension, but as she toweled her hair the bed looked very inviting. She was immensely tired. She knew she should be ecstatic. They had done all they'd set out to do. She had just won one of the top roping events in the country. There was no way anyone could keep this news from getting out. No way at all.

But instead of feeling happy, or even triumphant, she felt completely drained. She hung the towel over a chair and glanced at the bed again. She would just take a little nap before she went to meet the girls. They were busy celebrating, anyway. They'd be at it most of the night, probably.

She pulled back the covers and crawled into the bed. Stretching out on her back, she tried to blank her mind, to reach a deep level of relaxation. But Alex's face kept interfering. She sighed and opened her eyes. It was her own fault. She had put off thinking about him until after she'd done her job. Well, she was done now. And all the sadness and grief that she'd been holding at bay came bursting in on her. Tears coursed down her cheeks as she gave way to her feelings of loss. She had never known a man like Alex before. She missed him dreadfully.

She curled up in a little ball. How could he have asked such a thing of her? How could he have expected her to go back on her promise? There were no answers to these questions, of course, and, finally, cried out, she fell into a troubled sleep.

It took a few seconds for her mind to register the sound of the hesitant knock on the door. Still groggy, she reached for her robe and wrapped it hastily around her as she opened the door.

"What . . ." she began, but then words failed her. Alex Calloway stood outside the door, twirling his Stetson in nervous fingers. "May I come in?"

The sound of his voice brought a lump to her throat and she backed silently away to let him in, then numbly closed the door behind him. Still unsteady on her feet, she crossed the room and sank into a chair.

"Sit down," she said finally, the habit of politeness taking over. Her mind wasn't working right, she knew. He was here even though he'd said he was leaving. Beyond that fact she couldn't seem to think.

He perched on the side of the bed, tentatively, as though afraid he might have to leave in a hurry. "I . . . Congratulations," he said finally. "You did a great job."

She stared at him. "You saw?"

He nodded. "I . . . couldn't leave." He shook his head. "I started to. Even got in the car and drove for about fifty miles. But I couldn't go on. I had to be here. The thought that you might be hurt and I wouldn't even know it . . . I just couldn't stand it."

"I wasn't in any danger." For some reason his concern no longer annoyed her as it had.

"That's all right to *say*," he blurted out. "But when you love someone it's not so easy to *believe*. Especially after the accidents I've been seeing."

"When you love someone?" she repeated stupidly.

His eyes searched her face. "Like I love you."

For a second time, her heart seemed to stop, to stand still.

"You knew I loved you," he said. "That's what made me so mad when you wouldn't listen to me."

She shook her head. "Wait a minute. I didn't know. You never told me."

He sighed. "It seemed a little early to say the words. I had to get that Livingstone woman off my back. She threatened to sue me for breach of contract."

"Oh, no!"

He laughed bitterly. "Oh, yes. But my lawyer managed to take care of her. And I got the okay from my publisher for a new book." His eyes held hers. "That's why I asked you to meet me here. I'd hoped to have everything straightened out so I could propose." He sighed. "And then I saw you out there in the arena and I blew everything." He stood up. "I just wanted to apologize before I leave."

"Leave?" The word brought her abruptly to her feet.

"Yes. I knew it was wrong of me to ask you to give up what you were doing, what you believed in. I can't imagine how I could have been so stupid." He shrugged. "Raising girls doesn't necessarily make a man smart. So . . ."

He had taken to twirling his hat in his hands again. She took it from him and tossed it on the bed.

"You do understand that I couldn't have done anything else?" she asked. "That I gave my word and had to keep it?"

He nodded. "Yes, I understand."

"Then it doesn't have to follow that I don't care for you, just because I didn't do as you asked?"

"Of course not. How does that old line go? 'I could not love thee half so well, loved I not honor more'?"

"That's close enough," she said, moving nearer to him.

"You mean? . . ." He was trying to understand, wanting to believe.

She couldn't wait any longer. "I love you, Alex Calloway. I love you very much."

"You do?" Happiness battled with disbelief in his face.

"I do. Very much." And she stepped into his arms and raised her face for his kiss.

When he released her mouth, he pulled her down beside him on the bed and buried his face in her neck. "God, how I missed you! It was like I'd lost a part of myself."

"I know." She turned to face him. "It was that way for me, too."

"When can we get married?" he asked. "Have you any other commitments that must be met?"

"No," she said. "I've done what we set out to do. But your new book—you'll have to travel to do it."

"Not too far," he said, his mouth twisting in a grin, his eyes sparkling.

"Why not?"

He kissed the tip of her nose. "Because it's about women in rodeo."

"It is?"

"It is. And I've got a firm contract on it. There's just one hitch."

She knew it couldn't be too bad, not the way he was grinning. "I need a first-rate photographer to do some modern shots. And someone with the necessary know-how to help me dig up the old photos. Also," he said, his hand sliding inside her robe, "if this person happens to be small, strong and female, and very good in bed . . ."

Her body was responding to his touch. "Hmmmm," she said. "I think I have just the candidate for you."

"Good. We'll get married right away."

"Mom will need a little time," she reminded him. "She'll want a church wedding. I'm the only girl," she explained. "Besides, it'll help her get used to the idea that I won't be around anymore."

She sobered as she realized how much she would miss her mother and the West. But she had made her choice. She wanted to be with Alex, wherever he went.

"Emily." His voice had grown grave. "Are you figuring that we're going to travel a lot?"

She nodded.

"Then I guess I'd better tell you. I want to settle down. I'm tired of living out of a car. In fact, I'm looking for a place, or I was, until our misunderstanding."

She tried to take all this in. "Where?" she asked, praying silently that it wouldn't be in a big city.

"Near Jordan."

For a minute she couldn't believe her ears. Then she realized that he was watching her with concern.

"You aren't too disappointed, are you?"

"Disappointed!" she squealed, hugging him tightly. "How could I be disappointed when we're going to live in the most beautiful country there is? Oh, Alex, I can't believe it. I'm so happy." She snuggled against him contentedly. "So very happy."

"Me, too. There's just one more thing."

"Yes?"

"About your competing."

Her heart sank. She wasn't sure she could give that up right away.

"You've got to teach me how to drive that rig and do other things. I've got to be useful."

Her relieved laughter rang out. "You mean you'll want to come along?"

He scowled. "Of course I will. I've heard about those rodeo groupies. You think I'm going to let my wife roam around the country alone?"

He dropped the scowl and kissed her chin. "Seriously, Emily. I don't want our relationship to make either of us give things up. I want it to make life better for both of us."

"It will," she assured him, snuggling still closer against his side. "Oh, Alex, I'm so happy. Everything has turned out so well. I couldn't ask for another thing."

His lips brushed her ear and his hand cupped her breast as he whispered, "Let me go put the chain on the door. I'm sure you can think of something."

YOU'LL BE SWEPT AWAY WITH SILHOUETTE DESIRE

$1.75 each

1 ☐ James
2 ☐ Monet
3 ☐ Clay
4 ☐ Carey

5 ☐ Baker
6 ☐ Mallory
7 ☐ St. Claire

8 ☐ Dee
9 ☐ Simms
10 ☐ Smith

$1.95 each

11 ☐ James
12 ☐ Palmer
13 ☐ Wallace
14 ☐ Valley
15 ☐ Vernon
16 ☐ Major
17 ☐ Simms
18 ☐ Ross
19 ☐ James
20 ☐ Allison
21 ☐ Baker
22 ☐ Durant
23 ☐ Sunshine
24 ☐ Baxter
25 ☐ James
26 ☐ Palmer
27 ☐ Conrad
28 ☐ Lovan

29 ☐ Michelle
30 ☐ Lind
31 ☐ James
32 ☐ Clay
33 ☐ Powers
34 ☐ Milan
35 ☐ Major
36 ☐ Summers
37 ☐ James
38 ☐ Douglass
39 ☐ Monet
40 ☐ Mallory
41 ☐ St. Claire
42 ☐ Stewart
43 ☐ Simms
44 ☐ West
45 ☐ Clay
46 ☐ Chance

47 ☐ Michelle
48 ☐ Powers
49 ☐ James
50 ☐ Palmer
51 ☐ Lind
52 ☐ Morgan
53 ☐ Joyce
54 ☐ Fulford
55 ☐ James
56 ☐ Douglass
57 ☐ Michelle
58 ☐ Mallory
59 ☐ Powers
60 ☐ Dennis
61 ☐ Simms
62 ☐ Monet
63 ☐ Dee
64 ☐ Milan

65 ☐ Allison
66 ☐ Langtry
67 ☐ James
68 ☐ Browning
69 ☐ Carey
70 ☐ Victor
71 ☐ Joyce
72 ☐ Hart
73 ☐ St. Clair
74 ☐ Douglass
75 ☐ McKenna
76 ☐ Michelle
77 ☐ Lowell
78 ☐ Barber
79 ☐ Simms
80 ☐ Palmer
81 ☐ Kennedy
82 ☐ Clay

YOU'LL BE SWEPT AWAY WITH SILHOUETTE DESIRE
$1.95 each

83 ☐ Chance	100 ☐ Howard	117 ☐ Powers	134 ☐ McKenna
84 ☐ Powers	101 ☐ Morgan	118 ☐ Milan	135 ☐ Charlton
85 ☐ James	102 ☐ Palmer	119 ☐ John	136 ☐ Martel
86 ☐ Malek	103 ☐ James	120 ☐ Clay	137 ☐ Ross
87 ☐ Michelle	104 ☐ Chase	121 ☐ Browning	138 ☐ Chase
88 ☐ Trevor	105 ☐ Blair	122 ☐ Trent	139 ☐ St. Claire
89 ☐ Ross	106 ☐ Michelle	123 ☐ Paige	140 ☐ Joyce
90 ☐ Roszel	107 ☐ Chance	124 ☐ St. George	141 ☐ Morgan
91 ☐ Browning	108 ☐ Gladstone	125 ☐ Caimi	142 ☐ Nicole
92 ☐ Carey	109 ☐ Simms	126 ☐ Carey	143 ☐ Allison
93 ☐ Berk	110 ☐ Palmer	127 ☐ James	144 ☐ Evans
94 ☐ Robbins	111 ☐ Browning	128 ☐ Michelle	145 ☐ James
95 ☐ Summers	112 ☐ Nicole	129 ☐ Bishop	146 ☐ Knight
96 ☐ Milan	113 ☐ Cresswell	130 ☐ Blair	147 ☐ Scott
97 ☐ James	114 ☐ Ross	131 ☐ Larson	148 ☐ Powers
98 ☐ Joyce	115 ☐ James	132 ☐ McCoy	149 ☐ Galt
99 ☐ Major	116 ☐ Joyce	133 ☐ Monet	150 ☐ Simms

SILHOUETTE DESIRE, Department SD/6
1230 Avenue of the Americas
New York, NY 10020

Please send me the books I have checked above. I am enclosing $_____
(please add 75¢ to cover postage and handling. NYS and NYC residents please
add appropriate sales tax). Send check or money order—no cash or C.O.D.'s
please. Allow six weeks for delivery.

NAME _____

ADDRESS _____

CITY _____ STATE/ZIP _____

Coming Next Month

The Wrong Man by Ann Major

Grant and Abigail had loved each other years before, but he hadn't fit into her wealthy and privileged world. Now Grant was back—and though Abigail *knew* their love was still wrong, somehow nothing had ever felt so right.

Sweetheart Of A Deal by Suzanne Michelle

Tilley had left Wall Street for a calm life as a candy shop owner—and not even David Danforth was going to muscle her back into big business. Tilley set him straight, but found her life not nearly so sweet without his love.

Danielle's Doll by Angel Milan

Peter Weston was astonished to discover that his contractor "Danny" was all the woman he could want. Fighting for her child, Danielle didn't want his passion but found that caution didn't work in matters of the heart.

Promise Of Love by Ariel Berk

Carla's husband was gone, and she was sure she'd never love again—but Bryce Dalton aroused in her a desire she'd never felt before. Could this intensely passionate man banish her memories to let her reach out again?

Odds Against by Erin Ross

Schoolteacher Lori decided to play blackjack dealer for the summer, but found that her biggest challenge in the casino was vibrant Nick Minelli. Lori quickly learned how to gamble, but did she want to risk her heart against the odds?

Maid In Boston by Paula Corbett

Dairy farmer Kathryn hadn't thought she could be stirred by just the look in a man's eyes. She took the job in a big-city firm for excitement, but Mitchell Grant's particular brand just might be too hot to handle!